THE TWIG OF CYPRESS

The Twig of Cypress

by Lettice Cooper

IVES WASHBURN, INC.

NEW YORK

IVES WASHBURN, INC., *Publishers*
750 Third Avenue, New York, N.Y., 10017

THE TWIG OF CYPRESS

COPYRIGHT © 1965 BY LETTICE COOPER

FIRST AMERICAN EDITION

PUBLISHED BY IVES WASHBURN, INC., 1966

All rights reserved, including the right to reproduce
this book, or parts thereof, in any form, except for
the inclusion of brief quotations in a review.

29039

LIBRARY OF CONGRESS CATALOG CARD NUMBER: 66-22211

MANUFACTURED IN THE UNITED STATES OF AMERICA

To Juliet Piggott

CONTENTS

Author's Note

In the middle of the last century Italy was not one united country, as it is today, but divided into a number of separate states. Those in the north were mainly dominated by Austria; in the south, by France.

By this time, however, a strong movement had grown up, intent upon driving foreign rulers out of Italy and making the country free, united, self-governing. Many distinguished Italians contributed to this work. The Pope himself, Pius IX (*Pio Nono*), was one of the rulers in Italy, as well as head of the Church: he was liberal-minded and was at one time supposed to favor the movement. In fact, he withdrew his support and sided with the French. Another important figure, especially in the later history of unification, was the statesman Cavour, of the northern Kingdom of Piedmont. And there was Mazzini, who started the secret society known as *Giovine Italia,* or Young Italy. The young men who joined this were pledged to fight for the *Risorgimento* —the Resurgence of Italy.

Finally there was Garibaldi, who had campaigned in South America for the freedom of the new republics there, and who now returned to his homeland to make a passionate attempt to establish a united, free Italy.

The *Risorgimento* had its first real triumph before this story begins: the Pope and his French allies were driven from Rome, and a Roman Republic was declared. A government of three (a triumvirate) was elected by the people; one of these triumvirs was Mazzini. In the year 1849 the most important people in Rome were Mazzini, with what amounted to supreme political power, and Garibaldi, as general of the Republican forces.

Everyone knew that the French would return and try to recapture the city; and, in fact, Garibaldi and his forces opposed them in vain on the northwest boundaries. The brothers Strelli and their friends and relations are imaginary characters; and the Villa Manselli with its spy-tower is an invention of the author. All the rest is founded on history.

THE TWIG OF CYPRESS

I

A Secret

Italo woke in the dark, suddenly, as if an unusual noise had startled him. He raised himself on his elbow; the straw in the pallet on which he was lying creaked, but there was no other sound in the bedroom under the farmhouse roof which he shared with his two brothers. He sat up in bed rubbing the sleep out of his eyes. The window made a gray square in the blackness of the wall. Outside a light wind from the sea soughed across the fields and rustled the branches of the catalpa tree against the corner of the house.

Italo felt cold; he pulled the rough blanket up to his ears. He knew under his skin that something was wrong. Then he saw that the window was open. Who could have thought of opening it on a February night? But there was something else that was queer, and as he grew more wide awake he knew what it was. He could not hear the familiar and comfortable sound of his brothers' steady breathing in the room.

The pallet beside his was empty. Giovanni, the brother next in age to Italo, had gone away to be a sailor only a month ago. But why was there no sound from the other two beds where Marco and Bernardo slept? Italo got up and crept across the room. He cautiously put out a hand to Marco's pallet as he had sometimes done

1

when as a very little boy he wanted to feel the reassuring mound under the blanket. Now the blanket was stretched tight over the pallet. Marco was not there. Crawling across the bed Italo stretched out his hand to Bernardo's pallet against the wall. Here, too, there was only the flat blanket. Italo sat back on his heels shivering. Then the catalpa tree outside the window creaked loudly; the branches rustled against the wall as they did when a strong wind was blowing. But it was only a light wind. Someone was climbing up the catalpa tree. Someone was going to climb through the window into the room.

Italo's mind was still half dazed by sleep. He thought this must be a robber. He crept across to the window to shut it. He peered out, and could just see a big dark shape moving in the catalpa. His hand was on the window, when a familiar voice from the tree said, very low:

"Italo! Don't shut the window. It is us, Marco and Bernardo. Go back to bed."

Italo went back to his pallet but he did not lie down. He pulled the blanket up to his chin again, and sat staring through the dark. Now that he was no longer afraid he was curious. He always wanted to know things. He watched as first Marco, and then Bernardo, climbed through the window and slid down into the room.

"You *would* have to wake up," Marco whispered, as he gently shut the window.

"Where have you been?"

"That's nothing to do with you." Marco was the eldest of the young Strelli. He was nineteen. He expected the others to obey him without question, especially Italo, who was the youngest.

"Where have you been, Bernardo?" Italo whispered across the room.

Bernardo, who was not quite seventeen, was very

good-natured and not so far removed from the younger ones as Marco. He crept across the room and squatted by Italo's pallet.

"It's all right," he whispered. "It was only a bet. We had a bet with some friends of ours that we could go out at night and get back into the house without anybody seeing us. It was just a game. But you must not tell anyone, not Anita nor Clara nor Mamma, nor Papa. Certainly not Papa. I know you won't give us away, Italo. Will you promise?"

"I don't need to promise. I shouldn't tell about you. But I want to know . . ."

"Oh, you always want to know," Marco grumbled softly from his pallet.

"Well, I do. Which friends did you make the bet with? Was it the Crevi?"

"Listen, Italo," Bernardo said, "we can't tell you because it's a secret."

"I hate secrets," Italo grumbled.

"Never mind. You must keep this one for us. Lie down and go to sleep and forget about it, and I will lend you my clasp knife for the whole of tomorrow."

"You needn't try to bribe me," Italo muttered proudly. "I shan't tell about you." He added, "But I'd like to have the knife."

Bernardo's clasp knife, a town present from his Uncle Bibi in Rome, was the envy of all the Strelli brothers.

"All right, you shall have it if you won't lose it. Go to sleep now."

Bernardo went over to his pallet. The straw creaked as he threw himself down. A few minutes later Italo heard his deep breathing. Marco did not go to sleep so quickly. Italo heard him turn over this way and that for a bit, then he, too, was still and breathing deeply with an occasional snort.

3

Italo lay awake puzzling. His always active curiosity was aroused. He did not believe the story of the bet. It had not sounded true. What had Marco and Bernardo been doing? Had they been to see a girl? But Marco was in love with Giulia Crevi, in the farm on the hillside above Orlano, and went to see her openly by daylight. Had they been to play cards in the café at Pontevera? But they did that sometimes on a Saturday evening and there was no secret about it.

The room was growing warmer now that the night air was shut out. Italo snuggled down under his blanket, but he felt that he would never be able to go to sleep; he would lie awake all night wondering where his brothers had been.

It seemed to him that he had only been thinking this for a minute when he opened his eyes to find the room full of morning daylight, and to hear his father's voice shouting from the stairs.

"Marco! Bernardo!" he shouted. "Are you going to lie in bed all day? Do you expect me to do your milking for you?"

Marco and Bernardo scrambled up off their pallets, flung on their working clothes and went clattering down the staircase in their wooden clogs. Italo, too, got up. Now that Giovanni had gone a lot of small jobs fell to his share. His mother would expect him to fetch water for her from the well, and to bring in sticks for the fire.

Still puzzling about last night, Italo saw that Marco's other trousers and jacket were lying in a heap on the floor by his bed. Italo knew well enough that in a family of *contadini,* peasant farmers, clothes were hard to come by and had to be taken care of so that they would last a long time. He picked up Marco's trousers and hung them on the string stretching across one corner of the room which served for a wardrobe. He lifted Marco's

4

jacket from the floor. Something fell out of the pocket and he stooped to pick it up. It was a twig of cypress, green leaf and dark wood, about twice the length of his finger. Italo was just going to throw it out of the window when he heard footsteps noisily clattering upstairs, and Marco stood in the doorway. He saw Italo with the cypress twig in his hand. He sprang across the room.

"Leave that alone! Give it to me!"

"It's only an old twig of cypress," Italo said.

Marco snatched it and put it under his vest and shirt. He held his hand over it as if he wanted to keep it warm.

"Why must you always go nosing into everything?" His black eyes flashed at Italo, but Italo was used to Marco's sudden tempers and not much afraid of them.

"I was only putting away your clothes for you. Do it for yourself if you like."

"You keep to your own side of the room," Marco cried furiously. Then his temper went as quickly as it came. "Never mind, you meant no harm. Come down now, Mamma wants wood for the fire, and water, and I am busy. I have to mix a draught for one of the cows."

Italo followed his brother down the stairs. On the lowest step Marco paused and put a finger on his lips.

"Mind, not a word about last night."

"I promise," Italo said stiffly. He muttered to himself, "But I'll find out all the same."

Then, remembering that he was to have Bernardo's splendid knife for the whole day, he ran joyfully out to claim it.

2

At the Mill

Italo was playing ball with his sister, Anita, outside the kitchen door. Anita, who came between Italo and Giovanni in age, would not always play now. She helped her mother in the kitchen, and soon she was going to be apprenticed to a dressmaker in Pontevera. But this afternoon in the bright sunlight of early March she was a little girl again. She laughed and shouted and skipped into the air, her dark hair flapped on the shoulders of her old red dress, which was now so short for her that it hardly came to her knees. *Contadini* like the Strelli kept half the food they grew—the rest went to the bailiff for the landlord—and did not have to pay rent for their houses, but they earned hardly any money, and it was not easy to find clothes for six children who would keep on growing.

Rosa Strelli pulled back the curtain that covered the doorway of the kitchen.

"Where is Marco?"

She looked along the front of the house. It was all one building, living rooms at one end, hay loft and cart sheds in the middle, sheds for the oxen and cows and rabbits at the far end.

"Marco is sowing in the lower field, Mamma," Italo said.

"Bernardo, then? Someone must take a sack of grain to the mill. We are out of flour."

"Bernardo is mending one of the hen coops. We found a hole big enough for a fox to get through. Let me take the grain to the mill."

"Very well, but you must ask Bernardo to help you to lift the sack on to the cart. It is too heavy for you alone."

Italo was glad to have something to do. Some days he was very busy helping his father and brothers. Some days there seemed to be no work for him. Three sons were not really needed on the farm, and as soon as the Strelli had recovered from the effort of fitting out Giovanni to go to sea they would think of something for Italo. Italo was clever; he could read and write much better than any of his brothers. His parents even thought of asking Uncle Bibi if he could find some work for him in Rome a little later on. But Rome, from which the Pope had been driven out by the *Risorgimento,* the Italian Rising for Freedom, was a disturbed city in the spring of 1849.

Now Italo went into the stall and brought out Nello, one of the two big oxen, a beautiful white beast with large gentle brown eyes. Nello stood still while Italo put the harness over his broad back and buckled all the straps. Anita had gone to call Bernardo, who came and helped to yoke Nello to the cart, and hoisted the sack of corn on to it. Italo climbed importantly into the driving seat and gathered up the reins.

"Roberto at the mill will help you to lift the sack off the cart," Bernardo said.

"Don't loiter in Pontevera," Rosa called out. "I have not enough flour to make *pasta* for supper tonight. If you are not back in good time we shall all go hungry."

Italo shouted encouragingly to Nello, and drove off along the cart track. It was nice to be going to the mill on this sunny afternoon. He sometimes got tired of hanging about the farm. He envied Giovanni because he had gone off to see the world, and hoped that his turn would come soon. But he loved driving the ox cart, which he had only been allowed to do in the last year. He waved proudly to his father and Marco as he passed them sowing in the long field.

When he reached the mill, which was four miles away on the other side of the village of Pontevera, Roberto, the miller's son, came to help him to lift the sack off the cart. Roberto was about as old as Marco, and was rather a joke to the Strelli boys; he was such a fool. He had never been able to learn to read or write properly. Whatever anybody said to him surprised him so much that he listened with his mouth wide open, but he was very tall and strong. He hoisted the sack of grain on to his shoulder as if it had been a rabbit, and led the way into the millroom which was filled with the sound of running water.

"So *you*'ve brought the corn today, Italo," Roberto said.

"As you see."

"Where are Marco and Bernardo?"

"They are both working on the farm."

"Are they? Are they?" Roberto seemed to find this very surprising. He added, "But they are coming tonight?"

"Tonight? Where to?"

"Ah, *diamine!*" Roberto clapped his big hand over his mouth. "I forgot."

Italo as usual was curious. "What did you forget, Roberto?"

"Never mind," Roberto said hastily. "Of course, you are too young."

8

"Too young for what?"

"You mustn't ask me," Roberto said, and again covered his mouth and giggled.

"I am old enough to know anything that you know." Italo added in a coaxing voice, "Please, Roberto, tell me, where are Marco and Bernardo going this evening? I do so want to know."

Roberto shook his head.

"No, no; a young boy like you! If you want to know you must ask your brothers."

"Please, please, Roberto."

Roberto hesitated. He put his big floury hand in his trouser pocket and pulled out a battered twig of cypress.

"You've seen one like this?"

"Yes, yes. Marco has one."

"Oh, indeed, Marco has one." Roberto guffawed as if Italo had said something very funny.

"Why, Roberto? What is it? Tell me."

At this moment Roberto's father came into the millroom. Dino, the miller, was a big man like his son, but much brighter. He sometimes lost patience with Roberto.

He wiped the flour off his hand and offered it to Italo.

"Good afternoon, Italo. How are you? Are all well at home? Do not stand there chattering all day, Roberto. Rosa Strelli may be waiting for her flour, and Italo has a long drive home."

Italo squatted on the floor, rubbing the flour dust out of his eyes and watching as the two big round stones ground the corn between them, and the brownish gray flour poured out into a growing heap. He always loved watching this but today his mind was only half occupied with it. He was asking himself questions since at the moment there was no one else to ask.

9

"Where do Marco and Bernardo go?" he was asking himself. "What do they do? Why do they have these twigs of cypress?"

He hoped Roberto would tell him when he carried the sack of flour to the cart for him, but Roberto had grown cautious again.

"Don't ask questions," he said. "I haven't told you anything. You are too young. If Marco asks you, you must be sure and say I haven't told you anything." He laughed his loud, silly laugh. "I can keep a secret, can't I? As well as any of them. Yes, as well as any of them. Roberto can hold his tongue all right. You say that to Marco. Remember, I haven't told you anything."

"I don't believe you know any secrets," Italo taunted him.

"Oh, don't I?" Roberto hesitated, evidently tempted to prove that he did. Then he looked frightened again, "I haven't told you anything," he repeated.

"I can find out if I want to," Italo replied. He picked up the reins and shouted to Nello and set off for home.

3

Meeting by Moonlight

The dry stick under Italo's foot cracked like a whip. Italo dropped down on the rough grass between the olive trees. Sixty yards ahead of him in the open field Marco and Bernardo stopped, and looked behind them. The moon was full, the whole countryside was as clear as a map in the white light. Italo began to wriggle backwards on his belly. He knew where there was a hollow filled with last year's bracken leaves. If his brothers came back he could worm his way in there and curl up like a snake in its hole. Marco and Bernardo did not come back; they went on walking in single file along the narrow path at the edge of a ploughed field. Their tall shadows swooped across the ribs of turned earth. Italo moved cautiously forward and slid down into a dry ditch where the reeds came as high as his shoulder, so that by crouching a little he could walk under cover.

Where could Marco and Bernardo be going? They had passed the path that led into the Pontevera road, and the turning that led to the Crevi farm. They were on the crest of a low hill now and he saw their black figures cut out against the deep blue sky. That path led nowhere except to a few scattered farms where they had no particular friends. And of course to the ruined villa, the old villa that some Roman Senator long, long ago had built for his country house where he could spend the hottest part of the year away from the city. But that now was only a piece of wall and a jumble of broken stones. What could Marco and Bernardo want to go there for late at night?

Apparently that was where they were going. They skirted a farmhouse; a dog barked furiously, rattling his chain. He barked again as Italo stole past, and followed his brothers along the narrow path through the farmer's vineyard. Now Marco and Bernardo were on the cart track, and there was no cover to hide Italo if they looked round. The flat fields on either side of the track were cornfields. Italo fell a little further back and crouched down. If they saw him, and came back to find out who he was, they would send him home and tomorrow Marco would give him a beating. It would not be the first time he had been beaten for not minding his own business, but it never stopped him next time there was something that he wanted to know.

The wall of the ruined villa was in sight now, and the moonlight showed other figures besides Marco and Bernardo moving towards it. Italo decided that he had better wait and give them all a few minutes in which to get there. He lay down in a shallow ditch by the side of the cart track.

It was not long before he heard footsteps coming along the track. He flattened himself as much as he could, and pressed his thin body into the ditch. Two young men went past him, walking briskly and talking eagerly together.

"He is to bring a message from Garibaldi himself," he heard one of them say.

Italo stayed in the ditch until the young men had reached the end of the cart track and were walking up the gentle slope of the grassy hill on which the ruined villa stood. Then he stood up and ran to the end of the track. Now there would be no more ditches, no hiding places at all, only the exposed slope. He looked all round. Olive groves and vineyards, farms and plough-land and pasturage lay spread out under the moon, but he could not see another living creature stirring any-where in the countryside.

Italo knew that behind the villa there was a pathway half screened by bramble bushes which led up the slope toward a clump of cypresses growing just behind the re-maining wall. He skirted the mound at the base and crept up towards the villa by the bramble path. As he came near to the cypresses he could hear voices and see light shining over the top of the wall. He climbed very carefully; if a stick snapped under his foot here these people who had chosen such a secret meeting place could not fail to hear it. The path was rough and broken; in some places the brambles had grown right over it. They scratched Italo's legs and tore his hands as he pushed them out of his way. He took no notice. He could hear a man's voice speaking in the ruined villa, then a pause and several voices answering. He reached the top of the mound.

The cypress trees stood up black and tall against the moonlight. There was one place where their shadows fell across the wall. Italo made for this place, and felt about with his hands for a foothold. He found one and very cautiously climbed up till his chin was level with the highest stone. There were tufts of weeds growing everywhere along the top of the wall and these made a screen for him. He was able to balance himself on a jut-ting stone and look over into the partly enclosed space below.

The light came from what Italo recognized as one of their own stable lanterns. Marco was holding it at the elbow of a man who was sitting with some papers in his hand on a broken piece of stone column. Around them were grouped about twenty young men, most of whom Italo knew. He saw Bernardo, and Roberto from the mill, and Danielo and Lorenzo Crevi, and other grown-up sons from the *contadini* farms round.

The man sitting on the stone column folded up the paper in his hand and put it away in his pocket. He leaned forward, and Italo saw that he was wearing a red shirt which glowed in the light as the lantern swung round in Marco's hand. The man in the red shirt began to speak.

"Brothers, you have heard the Leader's, Garibaldi, message. What he says to you all is this: we who work for a free and united Italy are passing through difficult times. The Austrians occupy our country in the North; they have lately defeated the attempt of the King of Piedmont and Sardinia to drive them out of his province. They hold Venice, the pearl of Italy. The Pope has fled from Rome and at present the men of the *Risorgimento,* our men of the Freedom Movement, are in power in the city; but the French have sworn to come back and re-establish the Pope and the Government of the Papal States. Here in the kingdom of Naples the foreign King, the Bourbon, still rules. One day our beloved land will be free and united, Italy for the Italians. But before then, all of us, and especially you of Young Italy will have to suffer many dangers and hardships."

There was a murmur of agreement and approval from the young men squatting on the grass. One of them cried out, "What does Garibaldi want us to do?"

"Those of you who can should join him and his Italian Legion at Rieti. He has sent out a call for volunteers. Those who for some good reason cannot go should keep their eyes and ears open, should be ready to help friends or to harass enemies. Garibaldi wished me to tell you that you who take the twig of cypress are his children. He calls on you to be ready to live or die for the freedom of your country. He loves you all and wishes you well."

Again there was a subdued murmur of applause from the young men. Marco said eagerly:

"Fernando, say to Garibaldi that we are all Red-Shirts here even if we do not now wear them. We will be true to our oath, even if the red dye for our shirts has to come from our blood. Tell the General that we, too, love him, and that he will soon see some of us at Rieti."

"*Si, si,*" the others murmured. "True to our oath. At Rieti."

Marco, who seemed to be the leader of the group, lifted the lantern so that it shone on all of them and asked: "Are there any new members to be admitted this evening?"

Voices answered him. "*Si, si.* Ascanio, and Pietro here."

"Come forward, then," Marco said. "Who answers for them?"

Danielo Crevi lifted his hand. "I answer for Ascanio."

"And I for Pietro," another young man called out.

Marco beckoned. "Come here, then, Ascanio. Repeat the oath after me and take the twig of cypress."

Ascanio, a tall young man with a thin, eager face, stepped into the bright light round the lantern. With a quick movement Marco unfurled a small Italian flag, and held it flapping above them. He handed a twig of cypress to Ascanio to hold.

"Now say this: 'I dedicate myself in thought, word and deed to the purpose of establishing Italy as a united nation of free and equal men. I swear that I will be faithful to this purpose.' "

Ascanio repeated the words after Marco in a voice that trembled with excitement.

"The twig of cypress," Marco said, "is now yours. You are a member of Young Italy. You are our brother."

He embraced Ascanio as the others said in chorus:

"*Ora e sempre*. Now and for always."

"Come along, Pietro," Marco called.

Pietro, who was sitting on the outer edge of the circle, stumbled over a stone as he got up and did not appear for a few seconds in the ring of light round the lantern. Italo, enormously interested in all this, leaned over the top of the wall to see if Pietro was coming. His movement loosened the stone on which he was standing. It had probably been crumbling for years, and was not strong enough to stand his weight. Italo felt it giving way beneath his foot. He clutched at the weeds on top of the wall to prevent himself from falling. The stone on which he stood crashed down on the broken pieces at the bottom of the wall. The noise startled the men of Young Italy; it also startled Italo, who felt that the weeds were coming out of the stones in his grasp. In a desperate effort not to fall and make even more noise he threw his body half over the top of the wall. Some of the crumbling stones gave way beneath him, and before he could save himself he slid down with them into the circle of lantern light and rolled over at Marco's feet.

4

Italo Begs to Take the Oath

"A spy! A spy! A spy!"

Italo heard the word all round him as he lay on the ground with the breath knocked out of him by the fall. A hand gripped his collar and jerked him to his feet. The light from the lantern shining on his face half blinded him.

"Italo!" That was Marco's voice, astonished and very angry. Italo was getting his breath back. He wriggled and tried to break away from the hand that held him, but he was in a man's firm grasp. Fernando, the Red-Shirt, had him by the collar. Italo wriggled until he was nearly out of his own shirt, but Fernando only gripped him by the shoulder.

"Why, it's Italo! Italo Strelli! It's only young Italo!"

After all the other young men Roberto made the discovery.

"It's Italo, is it? Italo Strelli." Italo heard Roberto's loud guffaw of laughter.

"It's my young brother," Marco said to Fernando. Then, in the sharpest tone that Italo had ever heard from him, "What are you doing here, Italo?"

"I wanted to see what was happening."

"You should be ashamed," Marco said furiously.

"Wait a minute," Fernando said to Marco. He unloosed his grip on Italo's shoulder.

"Now, Italo, tell us how you knew about this meeting place. Who told you?"

"Nobody told me. I saw Marco and Bernardo going out and I followed them to see where they were going. They didn't see me. I was behind them all the way here."

"What did you do it for? Do you always follow your brothers when they go out without you?"

"No, but I knew there was a secret. I saw them come in one night, and Roberto told me that they were going somewhere tonight."

"Coming here?"

"He didn't say where. That was what I wanted to know."

Fernando said to all the young men, "You see how careful you must be. You must make sure that nobody sees you go out or come in again. But at least no great harm is done this time. It is a friend and not a spy who has found our meeting place. You are a friend to your brothers and to all here, is that not true, Italo?"

"Of course."

"And you understand that you must not tell anybody of what you have seen tonight?"

"I will tell nobody," Italo promised eagerly. "Why should I? I only wanted to know."

"Now that he does know," somebody said, "we shall have to find a new meeting place. He is too young to be trusted with our secret."

"No, I'm not. I can keep a secret as well as any of you." Hearing Roberto's guffaw again, Italo added resentfully, "As well as Roberto."

"What is the good of changing the meeting place?" somebody else shouted. "He knows us. He has heard the oath. He knows now which of us belongs to Young Italy. If he blabs a new meeting place will not save us."

18

"I shall never blab," Italo said. "I shall never speak a word of this. You can trust me."

"There are no traitors in the Strelli family," Marco said in a loud, clear voice.

"That's true." Bernardo supported him. Italo knew that however angry they were with him they were going to stand by him for the sake of family pride.

Danielo Crevi said, "It is not that we suspect Italo of meaning to betray us, but he is not old enough to remember to hold his tongue when he is playing about with other boys."

Suddenly Italo had an idea.

"Listen," he said. "I will prove that I am to be trusted and will not betray you. Let me take the oath! Let me join Young Italy! Give me the twig of cypress! Then your secret will by my secret, too, and you will know that if I betrayed you I should betray myself as well."

"He is too young to be a member of Young Italy," somebody muttered doubtfully.

"Wait a year or two," Roberto advised, with his silly laugh.

Marco turned on Roberto and said sharply, "It was from you that he heard that we were going out tonight."

Fernando spoke.

"I have often heard our Leader, Garibaldi, say that no one is too young nor too old to serve the cause of Italian freedom. Let Italo join us. Let him take the oath after Pietro and receive the twig of cypress, and have his name on our roll. He has offered to join us as a sign that he will keep faith with us. I think we should accept his offer. What do you all say?"

There was a general murmur of agreement.

"But first, Italo, I must make it quite clear to you what you are joining. Young Italy is a secret society with branches all over Italy. Its members are sworn, as you have heard tonight, to work for the freedom and unity of this country. They are part of the *Risorgimento*—the Awakening of Italy. Since Mazzini started the society twenty years ago many men have joined it. Sometimes they have been found out or betrayed. Many of the members of Young Italy have been arrested, imprisoned, tortured, killed. I am telling you this to show you that it is not a game we are playing. Sometimes when you are with your friends, boys of your own age, you may be tempted to tell them about it, or to hint that you know something exciting that they don't. If you do this, your brothers and their friends and you yourself will be in danger. Do you understand?"

"Yes. No one will find out from me."

"Very well, then. Wait while Pietro takes the oath and then it will be your turn."

Fernando picked up the flag again, and shook out its folds. As Pietro went through the ceremony that he had already watched when Ascanio performed it, Italo hugged himself with glee. Not only had he found out what he wanted to know, but he was to be admitted to this grand grown-up society: he would be able to steal out at night with Marco and Bernardo. Now they would be able to talk to him about it, and he could ask them more about this leader, Garibaldi. Italo had noticed before that when you found out about something it was seldom the end; it only meant that there were more things to find out. Who, for instance, was this Mazzini who had started Young Italy? Who had imprisoned and killed its members? The foreigners in Italy, he supposed. There were several things he would like to know.

"Come along, Italo."

Italo moved forward and stood in front of Fernando. Fernando put a twig of cypress into Italo's hand.

"Who answers for Italo?"

"I do," Marco replied.

"Repeat the words of the oath after me, Italo."

Trembling with excitement, Italo repeated: "I dedicate myself in thought, word and deed, to the purpose of establishing Italy as a united nation of free and equal men. I swear that I will be faithful to this purpose."

Fernando drew Italo towards him and kissed him on both cheeks.

"You have received the twig of cypress. You are now our brother."

The young men standing round said in chorus:

"*Ora e sempre.* Now and for always."

They all came up and shook hands with Ascanio and Pietro and Italo. Never in his life had Italo felt so grown-up. He put the twig of cypress inside his shirt where it tickled his chest. Roberto, as he came to Italo, seized his hand in his huge grasp and murmured:

"I didn't tell you anything, did I? I didn't tell you. But you found out. You know now." He chuckled as if this was very funny. Italo pulled his hand away. He felt that this was too serious to be one of Roberto's jokes.

Marco was the last to come to him. As he shook Italo's hand, he muttered, "I'll give you such a beating in the morning!"

Italo grinned. He knew that Marco was never angry for very long. His way was to beat at once or not to beat at all. Very likely by the morning he would have forgotten that he had ever thought of it. But even if Marco remembered, Italo felt that this evening's work would have been worth a beating.

5

Uncle Bibi

"Well, you're a skinny little lizard of a boy," Uncle Bibi said, giving a friendly tweak to Italo's ear.

"Italo is very strong," his mother said quickly, "and he is clever. Last week someone brought us a newspaper and he read it all through in two days. And he is very good at figures. He helps his father with the accounts."

"A student, eh? You have a fine family, Rosa, you and Matteo. I congratulate you both."

Rosa and Matteo Strelli looked very pleased. It was two years since Uncle Bibi, whose real name was Riccardo Fantoni, had been to the farm to see them, but he never forgot them. At Christmas he always sent greetings, and something for the twins, Clara and Bernardo, who were his god-children. This time he had brought a new shirt for Bernardo, and a length of flowered cotton print for Rosa and for each of the girls. Compared with the Strelli, Uncle Bibi was rich; he had a vegetable and fruit shop in Rome. It was particularly good of him to be so generous to them because he was not the children's uncle by blood. He had married their mother's sister, who had died ten years ago, leaving him with one son, Taddeo. Now Uncle Bibi had a new wife and a step-daughter, Zelinda, a year younger than Italo, but he never forgot his first wife's family.

"It does me good," he said, "to breathe this fine, fresh

country air after the close air of Rome. Let us have a look at your beasts, Matteo." He put a hand through his brother-in-law's arm and they walked off towards the sheds. Italo followed them. Uncle Bibi, coming from the city, was exciting because Italo might one day go to work there. Uncle Bibi could no doubt tell him all the things about living in Rome that he wanted to know.

"Are you coming with us, my little lizard?" Uncle Bibi said to Italo. "You will show me the new calf, eh?"

Nobody, Italo thought, could be less like a lizard than Uncle Bibi, who was more the shape of a wine barrel with two short stout legs underneath it, and a neck and bald head sticking out of the top. He had several gold teeth which Italo very much admired, and a round pale face and the brightest of twinkling brown eyes.

They went into the shed and admired the three days' old calf, a vigorous, curly-haired, black and white creature, already making skipping movements in the straw of the stall.

"A cow calf?" Uncle Bibi asked.

"No, alas, a bull. But Carolina there will calve in six weeks' time, and perhaps she will have a cow calf. We need another milk cow and if one is born the landlord will let us keep her. This one will have to be sold for veal as soon as he is old enough."

Italo plucked at Uncle Bibi's sleeve.

"Do you know what we are going to have to eat?" he whispered.

Uncle Bibi twinkled down at him.

"No. What?"

"A piece of meat from the butcher in Pontevera."

This was a great event. The Strelli hardly ever bought meat; they had their own rabbits and chickens on Sundays, and on weekdays they had spaghetti or macaroni or a maize porridge called *polenta*.

"I am sure it will be very good when cooked by your mother," Uncle Bibi said.

"Yes, it has basil and onions and tomatoes and rosemary with it in the pot. It smells wonderful when Mamma lifts off the lid."

They all went indoors and took their places at the long table in the kitchen, which was a big room covering the ground floor of the living part of the house. The end of it where they sat was quite cool today in spite of the warm April sunshine outside, and the fire well stoked up with wood at the other end of the room.

Matteo Strelli sat at the head of the table with Uncle Bibi on his right and Marco opposite to him at the bottom. Bernardo and Italo were on each side. Rosa and Clara and Anita waited on them. Afterwards, when the men had finished, the women would sit down at the table and have their own dinner. This was the custom in such farmhouses then, and nobody saw anything odd about it.

"I told you," Italo cried excitedly to Uncle Bibi, as his mother lifted the lid off the big pot and the delicious savory smell of meat and herbs and onions wafted across the room. Rosa ladled out huge platefuls and Clara and Anita carried them to the men at the table.

"There's no food like country food," Uncle Bibi said.

Italo plunged in his spoon and lifted as much as he could at once to his mouth. It was too hot to eat and he had to hold it up in the air to cool it. He laughed as if this was very funny. He was excited today, not only by Uncle Bibi's visit, but because Bernardo had told him that there was to be a meeting of Young Italy that night. This was the first meeting they had held since Italo had taken the oath, and he was looking forward to going out with his brothers after dark and climbing in at the window.

24

"And how are things in Rome?" Matteo Strelli asked his brother-in-law. Rome, though only eighteen miles away, seemed a long way off to him; he was not really much interested in what happened there, but it was a polite question to ask his guest.

"Everything goes very well," Uncle Bibi replied. "There were some who thought that after the Pope had fled and Mazzini was ruling the city all would be chaos, the Churches would be robbed, and no man would be able to go safely in the streets. But it is not so at all. The services in the Churches go on as usual and good order is kept everywhere. There is no difference between this new Government of the *Risorgimento* and the old one. I sell just as many fruits and vegetables—more, because the city is so full. But I don't know what we may have to put up with; they say that the French will bring the Pope back and restore him by force as the ruler of Rome. It will not be at all pleasant for us peaceful citizens if the French attack Rome and there is fighting. But perhaps some arrangement will be made and the Pope will be allowed to come back in peace."

"No," Marco said loudly. "He is the tool of the French. He cannot come back. And of course there will be fighting. Garibaldi will fight!"

"You are like all the young men," Uncle Bibi said placidly. "Like my own Taddeo. You make a saint and a hero of Garibaldi. Imagine, Taddeo has bought himself a red shirt. I have told him not to wear it in the shop. We do not know what will happen in the end and we have to sell our vegetables to all parties."

"Where is Garibaldi?"

"Still at Rieti. The Triumvirs will not allow him to bring his legion into Rome. They are afraid that he would cause too much disturbance with these wild Red-Shirts of his who have done so much fighting in Montevideo, in South America. People say that they are pirates and bandits, and that if they were allowed into the city we might all have our throats cut or our tills robbed."

"It is not true," Marco cried. "They are heroic soldiers, men who obey the discipline of their leader."

"Well, so Taddeo says. I am always half afraid that he may run off to join them. But he is a good lad and knows that I need him in our business now that I am getting older. If I were you, Matteo, I would not send Italo to Rome to look for work just now. I should wait and see how things go. He is very young. If there is to be fighting, as some people say, he would be better at home here until it is over."

"Oh, no, no," Italo cried. Every word that Uncle Bibi said made Rome sound more interesting.

"Silence, Italo," his father said severely. He thought Italo was much too fond of speaking up when he should be quiet and wait for his father to settle things for him.

Rosa Strelli, who was bringing some cream cheese that she had made by pressing sour milk into jars, said to Uncle Bibi, "If Rome is disturbed and there is fighting, you must send the little Zelinda down here to us until it is over."

When the men had finished eating, Rosa and the girls carried a flask of wine and some glasses outside and put them on the rough wooden table in the sunshine. Matteo and Uncle Bibi sat down and Marco with them. Bernardo went off to take the new calf out of his separate stall and to put him to feed from his mother. Italo went into the hen yard to collect the eggs. This was one of his jobs, but he had not done it that morning as he had gone with Bernardo in the ox cart to fetch Uncle Bibi from the coach stop in the village. There were some railways in Italy but they did not yet come to a small place like Pontevera.

Italo found seven eggs and then noticed a place where a fox had been scraping at the earth near the fence to try and get in. The fox had begun to make quite a hollow. Italo put the eggs carefully in the shade, and began to collect some earth to fill the hole. He was busy stooping over this when he heard a footstep on the path outside the fence, and a low whistle. He looked over the fence, and saw Danielo Crevi, who looked hot as if he had been hurrying.

"Italo, where is Marco?"

"Drinking wine with Papa and Uncle Bibi."

"Can you fetch him here? And Bernardo. Do not tell your father and your uncle. This is secret."

Danielo pulled back the front of his shirt, and touched the tip of his twig of cypress.

Italo nodded and flew off. He went first into the cowshed where Bernardo was just putting the calf back into his own stall.

"Come quick, Bernardo. Danielo Crevi is here. He wants you and Marco. It is something secret."

Bernardo shut the door on the calf and latched it. "Where is Danielo?"

"At the back by the hen run."

"I am coming."

Italo ran across to the table where the three men were drinking their wine. He caught hold of Marco's elbow.

"Marco, will you come? A fox has been making a hole underneath the fence round the hen run."

Marco, who was still young enough to enjoy being a man with the older men, shook Italo off.

"I'll come later. The fox will not try to get in by daylight with you about there."

"Marco," Italo said desperately, "it is a big hole. I think we ought to try and fill it up with some twigs of cypress."

Marco drank off the half glass of wine in front of him and got up. He said to his father, "I will just see this hole, and come back."

Matteo nodded. As a matter of fact he and Uncle Bibi would be quite glad to get rid of all the young ones and talk over their own affairs in peace.

Marco moved off quickly, but he said over his shoulder to Italo. "Are you playing a trick?"

"No. Danielo Crevi is here. He sent me to fetch you and Bernardo about something to do with this." He showed the tip of his twig of cypress.

Marco said nothing, but he walked faster with his long strides and Italo trotted after him.

Danielo Crevi and Bernardo were sitting on the ground near the fox's hole. Danielo jumped up and came to meet Marco.

"Marco," he said. "There must be no meeting tonight. There are soldiers of the Neapolitan Army now hidden in the ruined villa. Benedetta saw them. She went that way with another girl to pick flowers. The soldiers are lying under cover in the ruins; they are waiting for Young Italy. Somebody has betrayed us!"

6

The Corporal's List

"It wasn't me," Italo exclaimed. "I haven't said a word to anyone."

"We haven't time now to think who it was," Marco said. "The others must be warned."

"Lorenzo has gone to the farms on the other side of Pontevera," Danielo said. "Benedetta went to the mill to tell Roberto. One of us must go on now to the Prati at Orlano."

"I'll go," Bernardo offered.

Danielo Crevi nodded. "Then I can go back by the Solti farm and tell Fabio, and I think that is all. If they know our names, Marco, they may come looking for us to arrest us."

"I'd thought of that," Marco said grimly.

Danielo spread out his hands. "Well, what will be will be. We shall have to dodge them as we can. *Addio*."

Danielo and Bernardo sped away in different directions.

"What shall we do?" Italo asked.

"We'd better finish stopping this hole before the fox comes again tonight."

"But I mean about . . ."

"Nothing we can do at the moment."

As they carried earth and stones towards the fence,

Italo said, "You know it wasn't me, don't you, Marco? You don't think it was?"

Marco gave him a long look.

"No, I trust you, Italo."

Italo glowed with warmth.

"Know who I think it was? I think it was that fool Roberto. He nearly told me about it the other day."

"It could have been. I never wanted him in. But I don't know why he should want to betray us. Roberto is a fool but he is very good-natured."

Italo knelt to push a stone in underneath the fence where the fox had scraped away the soil. Marco stamped down the earth with his clogs. They both stood up and both exclaimed. Along the cart track that led to the farm a small party of soldiers was riding.

"Quick. The cave," Marco said. "Keep your head down, then the fence will hide us."

Marco ran up the hillside and Italo scampered after him. The cave was an old hiding place, a hollow in the hillside above the olive grove where the four boys had dug out the soft earth and made a screen of wood and trained honeysuckle and brambles to grow over them. It had been their private place for hiding when they wanted a day off from school, or were escaping from some job on the farm that they did not want to do.

Italo dodged after Marco between the olive trees. They pulled aside the trailing branches that had grown over the opening, and flung themselves down panting on the floor of the cave. Italo peered through the tangle of budding twigs that sheltered the front of their hiding place.

"Can you see them?"

"No, they must be in front of the house now. It hides them from us."

Uncle Bibi and Matteo were startled when they

turned round suddenly from their wine and saw a Corporal and six soldiers, cavalry of the Neapolitan Army, riding up to the house. The Corporal dismounted and gave the reins of his horse to one of his men. He came across to the table under the tree. He was a young man with a red face and a plump neck for which the braided collar of his uniform coat seemed too tight. He had small, beady black eyes. He looked at a list in his hand.

"You are Matteo Strelli?"

"Yes."

"You have three sons?"

"I have four, but one has gone to sea."

"He is in the Royal Navy in the service of his Majesty the King of Naples," Uncle Bibi said quickly.

"It only says three here." The Corporal consulted his list again. "Here are Marco, Bernardo and Italo. And they are members of the secret society, Young Italy?"

"Certainly not," Matteo replied. "They are not members of any society. They are *contadini*. They work here with me on the farm. At least, Italo may go away later to other work, but at present he helps me and his brothers."

"But there is a branch of Young Italy here," the Corporal persisted. "They meet in the ruined villa at night. Your three sons go to the meetings?"

"How could they go to any meetings at night without my knowing? The door of the house is bolted at nightfall."

"Their names are down here," the Corporal said in rather a puzzled way. "Where are they?"

"They will be somewhere about the farm. They went to mend a fox hole under the fence round the hen yard."

"We must search for them."

"Signor Corporal," Uncle Bibi interrupted, "you

31

have had a long dusty ride. Could you not sit down and drink a glass of wine with us while your men search?"

The Corporal looked at the big wicker-covered flask of wine and at the chair Marco had left.

"Well, perhaps. Thank you." He turned to his men. "Dismount and tether your horses. Look round the farm and in the house for the three sons. Be sure and look in the hayloft. Turn the hay well over."

"I will fetch a clean glass," Uncle Bibi said quickly. He went into the kitchen and Matteo saw him speaking to Rosa just inside the door. He came out quickly again. The Corporal sat down and Matteo filled his glass.

"Your health," the Corporal said, bowing to Matteo. "You understand me. I myself have nothing against these young men. In fact I admire Garibaldi, though of course I would not say so in the barracks except to my own close friends, you understand, who admire him, too. After all, we are all Italians. There are too many foreigners in our country."

The Corporal drank off his wine, and smiled as the cool liquid went down his dry throat. Uncle Bibi at once refilled his glass.

"It is hardly work for soldiers," Uncle Bibi said, "to go about the place arresting young men who may not, after all, have done anything wrong. It is work for the police, I should have thought."

"That is what I say," the Corporal agreed. "And lately we have not had to do this so often. They think about it at one time, those in authority, you know, and then they forget. To tell you the truth," the Corporal winked at them, "there are those in authority who do not much care for Bomba. That is what we call this Bourbon king of Naples they have put to rule over us, you know, Bomba. I believe there are people in high places who drink a health to Garibaldi now and then when they are alone, in good company, you know."

He winked again and drained his glass. Uncle Bibi filled it up once more.

"You do not live on the farm?" the Corporal said to Uncle Bibi.

"No, I am only here on a visit to my family. I live in Rome."

"Aha, we are men of the world, you and I," the Corporal chuckled. "This is excellent wine."

"It is from our own vines," Matteo said, with pride.

"I hope," Uncle Bibi said, "that your men will soon find the lads. When you see them you will understand how very unlikely it is that they should be members of a secret society. Why, Italo, the youngest, is only twelve. I do not think any political society would include boys of that age. In fact, if you ask me I think the whole thing is a hoax. Somebody has been pulling the leg of your officers."

"Certainly somebody came to the camp with information and this list," the Corporal said doubtfully. "But it would be a wicked hoax; these lads might get into serious trouble."

Uncle Bibi said nothing. He was watching as a soldier's head appeared here and there above the fence, a blue and red uniform showed between the olive trees. Uncle Bibi wiped the sweat off his bald head.

"It is hot," he said, "for April. Let me give you some more wine, Corporal."

A soldier called out to Clara, who stood in the doorway, to find him a pitchfork and show him the way up to the hayloft.

"Matteo," Uncle Bibi said, "would it not be a good thing for you to go and show the soldier where to find what he wants?"

Matteo went off. He did not half understand what the

whole thing was about. Of course his sons would not belong to any political society without his knowing about it. He did not like the soldiers coming after them; it made him very uneasy, but not as uneasy as he might have been because he was so sure that it was a mistake. He was very glad that Bibi was here. It had been a good idea to make the Corporal drink with them. Bibi knew how to handle things. Matteo went into the stables and found the soldier a fork. He climbed up after him into the hayloft and stood watching him while he turned over the heaps of dry hay.

"What do you think you will find there?" Matteo asked him. "A lark's nest, perhaps?"

Outside, Uncle Bibi said to the Corporal, "You are a fine young man. I feel very sorry for you because your officers have sent you on a wild goose chase, and perhaps they will be angry with you when you go back to the camp and tell them there is no secret society here."

The Corporal laughed. "What, on Saturday night? They won't care. They'll all be off to their pleasures in Naples."

"So you will have had all your trouble for nothing. And your men will grumble all the way home. It would be better if you could take them to the Café at Pontevera and buy them some wine to get the dust out of their throats."

"It would certainly be better," the Corporal said, laughing. "But I'm a poor man, I send half my pay home to my old mother and sometimes even my pay is in arrears."

Uncle Bibi took a fat purse out of his pocket. "The wine would be at my expense."

"You are very generous."

The Corporal's beady eyes grew brighter as he saw how much money Uncle Bibi was holding in his hand.

34

"I just want you to do one thing for me," Uncle Bibi said. "Only one little thing."

"It will be a pleasure."

Uncle Bibi said, in a tone that was firmer and less coaxing, the tone of a man clinching a bargain. "I want that list."

The Corporal hesitated. He knew that half the army of the King of Naples, officers and men, sympathized with the *Risorgimento*. He knew that his own Lieutenant was not in the least interested in rounding up the members of Young Italy. If they were caught they would have to be punished, but most people would prefer not to catch them. If he went back to the camp and said that the whole thing had turned out to be a hoax, nobody would care, nobody would want to see the list of names again. But this fat man from Rome wanted the list and was willing to pay money for it, so perhaps the Corporal could make him pay more money.

He said in a doleful voice, "If I do not bring the list back I shall get into trouble." He looked at the money in Uncle Bibi's hand.

Uncle Bibi was a business man. He did not want to pay more for anything than it was worth.

"I should not like you to get into trouble," he said. He began to put the money away in his purse again.

The Corporal was alarmed. "I do not say that it is impossible that you should have the list," he said hastily. "But I have to think of what my officers will say."

Uncle Bibi began to put the purse back in his pocket.

"Take it," the Corporal said, holding out the list. "After all, I do not want to get honest *contadini* lads into trouble."

Uncle Bibi took the list and opened the purse again. "You may as well take your men back to camp now," he said, "since it is only a hoax."

The Corporal pocketed the money. *"Si, Signore,* I am going."

He stood up and shouted. His men, who were tired of searching and finding nobody, came running. "We have been given some false information," the Corporal said to his men. "There are no members of Young Italy in these parts. We will ride now to Pontevera and call at the café for a glass of wine on our way through."

Uncle Bibi looked at the list. It was printed in large capitals, so it was no good keeping it to find out who had written it. He tore it slowly into tiny pieces. He kicked a hole in the ground with his heel and put the scraps of paper in and covered them and trod them down. He said to himself, "The silly lads! May the Holy Saints send someone to protect my Taddeo if he should ever be in the same danger."

When Matteo came back from the house Uncle Bibi shook his finger at him.

"What is the use of stopping the holes by which foxes get in if you do not even know the hole by which your sons get out? Of course they have taken the twig of cypress! No, it is no use beating them. If we were young men now we should probably do the same. It is in the air, you see, this wish to fight and struggle for Italy and freedom. There is nothing we old ones can do to stop it. Often," Uncle Bibi added, "I wish I were young. Come, let us find the boys and tell them that for the moment they are safe."

Matteo, looking half angry, half puzzled, followed Uncle Bibi up the hillside.

7

Suspicion

"Italo! Italo!"

Italo was helping Bernardo to clean the cowshed and put down fresh straw for the beasts. He ran out when he heard his mother calling from the kitchen doorway.

"Italo, will you take my plants to Pontevera, to the church? They will have to go in the handcart. There are one or two things I want from Enrico's, and you had better make your Easter confession while you are at Pontevera. Father Anselmo will be in the church all day, and it will save you having to go in again this evening."

It was the Saturday before Easter, and everyone was busy getting the house and the farm ready for tomorrow's holiday. Italo was quite willing to go into Pontevera; there was always a chance he might see or hear something interesting.

"Oh, how beautiful the plants are!" he exclaimed. Rosa Strelli grew lilies in pots every year specially for the church at Easter. She kept them warm inside the kitchen and watered them and cherished them, so that now she had nine pots with white lilies in flower long before they were out in any of the gardens.

"You will be very careful of them," she urged, as they lifted the heavy pots into the cart and put pieces of wood and bundles of straw in between to wedge them firmly. "Keep the cart in the middle of the track so that the wheels don't catch in the ruts at the side and upset the pots."

She gave him some money with which to buy salt and soap and a reel of strong black cotton. "And there will be a little over so you can buy an ounce of sweets for yourself and Anita for Easter."

This was a rare treat. Italo set off in high spirits, pushing the cart very carefully and steadily along the middle of the cart track. He felt relieved when he reached the smoother surface of the road, although even here there were a lot of hollows and he had to be careful of bumps and jolts.

He got all the lilies safely to the village and wheeled them to the doorway of the church. He pushed aside the heavy red curtain hanging over the door, and went in. At first, as he came from the bright sunlight outside to the dim brown light of the church, he could not see anything. He sniffed the smell of incense, which he liked, and peered about him. Then he saw Father Anselmo who was spreading a clean embroidered linen cloth on the altar. Hearing Italo's footsteps the priest turned and came down the church to meet him.

"Father," Italo whispered, "I have brought the plants for the church from my mother. And will you please hear my Easter confession?"

"Shall we bring the plants in first?" Father Anselmo suggested. "It will be better than leaving them out in the sun."

Between them they carried the heavy pots into the church and up the aisle.

"How beautiful they are," the priest said. "Your mother is a good daughter of the Church. She gives us of her best every year, but I think these are the most beautiful she has grown yet."

He and Italo arranged the pots round the sides of the altar so that it looked as if it stood in a bed of lilies. They went back to the other end of the church to admire the effect.

"And now, my son," Father Anselmo said, "you had better kneel down for a few minutes and prepare yourself for your confession."

The priest disappeared into the confessional box at the side of the church. After kneeling down with his eyes tightly shut for a minute or two Italo went up and took his place on the kneeling stool in the box, where a partition separated him from the priest.

Confession was always rather frightening. Father Anselmo inside the box with only his eyes showing through the hole was no longer the priest who had baptized Italo, and who came sometimes to the farm and ate and drank wine with them and made little jokes. He became more like a terrible angel on the day of judgement.

"Have you anything else you want to tell me?" he asked when Italo had finished.

Italo racked his brains. It was always very hard to remember his sins. He had confessed about leaving the door of the calf's stall open so that he got out, and was only just headed off from rushing among the young vines. He had told about the time he had quarrelled with Anita and made her cry. He had told how, when his mother asked him to bring the washing in because it was raining, he had grumbled and said that it was a girl's job. He had told of stealing after Marco and Bernardo to find out about the secret meeting. He really could not remember anything else.

"That is all, Father."

"You are quite sure, my son?"

Italo could see Father Anselmo's eyes looking at him very hard through the hole. The priest said, "There is nothing else that you want to tell me? Nothing that has been worrying you since you went to the secret meeting?"

"No Father."

"Very well, my son."

Father Anselmo gave Italo the absolution and the blessing and told him to say two extra Pater Nosters and two Hail Marys before he went to sleep that night.

Pleased to have got that over, and to be forgiven for all his sins, Italo took one more proud look at the lilies and skipped out into the sunshine.

The village shop, kept by Enrico, was also the village café. There were tables outside under an awning of vines and wistaria. Italo had never sat at one of these tables to drink wine or coffee; he never had any money of his own. He saw now that Roberto from the mill was sitting there with his cousin Benito Lupini, who was a clerk in a government office in Albano, six miles away.

Benito had a good job. He was always rather grand in a town suit, and always had money to spend. He and Roberto were sitting with two full glasses of wine on the table in front of them. Benito patronized Roberto, who did not seem to mind but was proud of his worldly cousin. Italo did not think that Benito was anything to be proud of, not to be compared with his own two elder brothers, but he thought that Roberto was too stupid to see that his cousin gave himself airs and half despised him.

Italo saluted them politely on his way to the shop.

"*Ciao*, Roberto. *Ciao*, Benito."

There were several people in the shop buying things and of course Italo knew most of them. He said, "*Ciao*," to them, too. One old woman answered him. The two Fredi brothers, *contadini* from one of the Orlano farms, turned their backs on him and began to talk hard to each other about some cord they were buying. A girl

40

who had been at the village school with Italo smiled faintly and then quickly looked away.

Italo went to the counter, and Enrico came to serve him, but he did not look at Italo's face. He did not ask him how his mother and father were. He seemed flustered; Italo had meant to examine all the sweets in their bottles carefully before deciding, but he too began to feel flustered though he didn't know why. He hastily chose aniseed balls, and took up his parcel. He said, *"Ciao,"* to Enrico and to the others and went out, quite glad, though again he did not exactly know why, to find himself outside the door.

Roberto and Benito were still sitting there. Roberto waved his big hand to Italo with a beckoning gesture.

"Come here, Italo. Come and drink a glass of wine with us."

Nobody had ever asked Italo to sit down at the tables and have a drink before. He said, "Thanks, Roberto," in a careless way as if it happened to him every day, and sat down opposite to Benito. Benito had a pale face, a long, thin nose and a slight squint as if his eyes were trying to meet across his nose.

"We need some more wine," he said. "Is there no waiter?"

"No, of course not," Roberto answered. "You know there is only Enrico and sometimes Giulia when she can leave the children. When Enrico is busy, we have to serve ourselves."

"This sort of thing would not do in Albano," Benito said in a scornful way. "But I will go and fetch the wine."

When he had gone Roberto looked at Italo and closed one eye in a laborious wink.

"So you found out, eh?" he said. "I shall never forget how funny you looked when you rolled into the middle

41

of the meeting. I can see it now." He laughed and Italo scowled at him. "Tell me," Roberto leaned nearer to Italo, "did Marco beat you for this?"

"The morning after the meeting? No."

"No, I mean after the soldiers came to look for us."

Italo stiffened. "Why should he?"

"Well, I thought . . . but, after all, as Benito has just said to me, nobody could expect a boy as young as you to hold his tongue. Benito said he was sure you meant no harm."

"What do you mean, Roberto? What have you been saying about me, you and Benito?"

Italo sounded so fierce that Roberto drew back.

"Nothing, nothing. Benito was sorry for you. He said he should not care to be in your shoes."

Benito came back to the table carrying three glasses of wine. As he sat down Italo stood up.

"Benito, have you been saying that it was I who told the soldiers about the secret meetings?"

"Now, let's forget about all that," Benito said soothingly. "It's over and no harm done. Roberto and I are not among those who are angry with you. At your age, what could anyone expect of you? Sit down and drink your wine . . ."

"No!" With his hand Italo swept the glasses off the table. They fell on the trodden earth. One of them smashed; the others rolled under the table.

"I told no one," Italo said. "Whoever went to the soldiers, it was not me. You are a liar, and Roberto is another. I shall tell my brothers."

He walked away from them, picked up the handles of the cart and began to wheel it home. Roberto and Benito called after him and he heard Roberto's great rumble of laughter. He walked on without turning round.

But he felt more angry and miserable than he had ever felt in his life. They thought that he had betrayed Young Italy. Everybody in the district probably thought so. It was terrible. He could never go to Pontevera again, never see any of the young men from the other farms, unless he or Marco and Bernardo could make them understand that he had not breathed a whisper of the secret meetings. They thought he had done it because he was only a boy and because they had caught him listening to their secrets. Perhaps even the priest thought so and that was why he had asked again if Italo had anything more to confess.

The Strelli were a family who had lived for many generations on their farm, and whom everyone respected. Italo, without thinking about it, had grown up knowing this, feeling himself a part of something good. Now everyone thought him a traitor. He could not bear it! Tears ran down his cheeks as he pushed the cart along the lane and along the cart track. The sun was very hot on his back and the road very dusty. He could never remember that it had seemed to take such a long time to get home.

He wanted to see his brothers but they were all out in the fields. Only his mother was in the kitchen, plucking a pair of hens for the Easter Day dinner. She looked up over the heap of feathers and asked at once, "What is it, my little one?"

Italo flung himself into her lap, and told his story. Of course, Rosa Strelli knew now that her sons belonged to Young Italy and had been stealing out at night to secret meetings. It had all come out after the soldiers' visit, when Uncle Bibi was there.

"If I only knew *who* told," Italo said. "If I could only find out *who*. Then I would tell everyone and they would all know it wasn't me."

43

"You must be patient, *piccino*," Rosa Strelli said. "I am sure that many people, the Crevi for instance, know that you would never do such a thing. We all know how foolish Roberto is."

"Yes, but it wasn't only Roberto and Benito. Enrico and the people in the shop wouldn't speak to me."

"They will forget, and perhaps there is something we can do. I will talk to Father Anselmo. He knows us well and trusts us. He can talk to the others."

"Speak to him today," Italo urged. He felt that he could not live in this undeserved disgrace any longer.

He was unhappy all the weekend. His mother did as she promised and spoke to the priest, who warned the village in his sermon on Sunday about making hasty judgments, and promised to speak to Roberto.

On Monday afternoon Marco was missing from the farm. He did not come home in time for the milking. Bernardo and Italo had to get all the food in for the beasts and shut up the hens for the night. They were just coming back to the house when they saw Marco walking up the cart track towards them. He had a big bruise on his forehead, and walked rather stiffly, sucking the bleeding knuckles of one hand.

"There will be no more trouble from Roberto," Marco said to Italo. "I have given him two black eyes. He won't see out of them till the end of the week."

That night Rosa Strelli said to Matteo, "I am afraid of this, I do not know where it might end. I think we should write a letter to Bibi, and ask him to let Italo come to him now to look for work in Rome."

44

8

Rome

"Is this all Rome?" Italo asked in astonishment.

"This is only part of Rome," Uncle Bibi answered.

Italo looked at the crowded pavement, at the tall houses, and at the carriages and cabs and horses passing in the street.

"How many people live here?"

"Nearly 180,000. Some have gone away at the moment because they think that the French are going to attack the city. But then a lot more have come in to help defend Rome against the French. Taddeo leaves me today to join Garibaldi's volunteers."

"Oh! Then I shan't see Taddeo."

"Yes, he is waiting to leave until he has welcomed you. You will find your Aunt Maria and Zelinda very sad, but it will cheer them up to see you."

"Who are those?" Italo cried out. Two men were coming towards them wearing red shirts and broad-brimmed cowboy hats with black plumes. They were bearded and their hair hung down to their shoulders.

"Those are two of the Tigers of Montevideo, Garibaldi's own Italian Legion who fought under him in Montevideo, in South America. The Triumvirs have only just allowed them to come into Rome. They thought that they would be wild and undisciplined and frighten the people. But now there is more reason to be frightened of the French, so the Tigers are welcome, and they have given no trouble."

Italo shifted his bundle of clothes to his other arm. Uncle Bibi, rolling along beside him, was carrying the presents Italo had brought from the farm, a big flask of wine made from the Strelli grapes, and a flagon of oil from their olives.

"I wish I could go with Taddeo and be a Tiger of Montevideo!" Italo sighed.

"Taddeo won't be that. It is only the old soldiers of the Legion who have that name, but the volunteers are all called Red-Shirts now."

Italo began to lag behind Uncle Bibi. There were so many exciting people and things to look at. Two priests in long brown cassocks went past them; then a nun whose black robes swept the dusty pavement while she held out her begging box, repeating, "For the poor, *signori*. For the poor." Uncle Bibi dropped in a small coin. A carriage went by in which sat a man in a black frock coat and top hat, a broad red, green and white ribbon across his breast.

"That is one of the Triumvirs, one of the men elected to rule the city instead of the Pope's government," Uncle Bibi explained. "Are you tired, Italo? We are nearly there."

"No, thank you, I am not tired." It was just that he couldn't hurry while there was so much to look at. His energy seemed to go into his eyes instead of into his legs.

"Where shall I find work here?" he asked. He thought that it would be bewildering to know where to begin looking for it in this huge place.

"You will not need to look for it just yet. You can help me with the shop while Taddeo is away."

46

"Oh, yes, I will," Italo said eagerly. What a relief to be able to work for kind Uncle Bibi instead of having to find a job among strangers!

An officer passed them wearing a dark uniform, and a round, brimmed hat with a tuft of dark green blackcock's feather in it.

"Is that another Tiger?"

"No, that is an officer of the Bersaglieri, the trained soldiers of Piedmont in the north who have come down here to fight for Rome."

"They will win, won't they?" Italo asked confidently.

"I don't know. The Tigers and the Bersaglieri and the National Guard altogether are not as many as the French troops. The French have one of the finest armies in the world, and our volunteers have not yet seen any fighting."

"What will happen if the French win?"

"Then they will put the Pope and his government back again in Rome." Uncle Bibi spoke seriously. He was thinking about Taddeo, who would be fighting in his first battle without any military training. Then he looked down at Italo's black head bobbing beside him, and said, "But, anyhow, people will always want fruit and vegetables, and you and I will work together to supply them."

When they reached the shop, which was at the corner of a street and of a square of old houses in the Trastavere, they saw Taddeo in his red shirt selling oranges to a group of women. The time had passed when it was wiser for a shopman not to wear a red shirt in Rome. Now people were all the more ready to buy from one of their defenders.

Taddeo could not leave the customers he was serving, but he waved to Italo and smiled at him. Taddeo was like his brother Marco, tall and lithe, with black hair and eyes, but his eyes did not flash so brightly. He had a gentle face.

"Come in this way," Uncle Bibi pushed open a door at the side of the shop, which led straight on to a narrow flight of stairs. Uncle Bibi hoisted himself up these, grunting. Italo followed him lightly. A woman's voice called from the top.

"Is that you, Bibi? Have you brought the little one?"

"Yes, here he is." Italo, who hardly remembered his Aunt Maria, found himself gathered into the arms of a plump, rosy, brown-haired woman who embraced him warmly.

"*Ecco!* Here he is. Zelinda, your cousin Italo."

Italo had not seen his cousin Zelinda since she came to stay at the farm six years ago when she had been a round little person of five. Now she was a long-legged girl of eleven, rosy and brown like her mother. She, too, embraced Italo. He saw that both Aunt Maria and Zelinda had been crying.

"You have heard," Aunt Maria said at once, "that our dear Taddeo goes this afternoon to join Garibaldi? And that in the next day or two they may have to fight the French? Ai!" She began to cry again, and then hastily wiped her tears away with the corner of her black apron. "But you have had a journey, Italo dear, you must be tired and hungry and thirsty. Bibi, it is almost one o'clock. Let Zelinda run and tell Taddeo to shut the shop. Let us all have a last meal together. I have made *gnocchi Romani,* which Taddeo loves, and we will drink this good wine which Rosa and Matteo have sent us. Ah, how fortunate they are that they have their Marco and Bernardo at home in the country with them and that Italo is too young to fight! You see, Italo, we are all one family here. Taddeo has always been as my own son to me, and Bibi is a father to Zelinda. And now you will be our son, too, and help Bibi until Taddeo comes back from the fighting. If he ever does." She began to cry again, but Zelinda was looking at her new cousin, Italo, with so much interest that her tears had dried.

"*Chut*," Uncle Bibi said, "do not let us expect the worst. Let us make this a little feast to send Taddeo off in good spirits and to welcome Italo. Zelinda, dear, will you ask Taddeo to bring up from the shop some of the best grapes and oranges, and a lemon to dress the salad with? Ask him to put up the notice that we shall be open at three as usual. Italo and I will then take charge."

As Zelinda pattered down the steep stairs, Italo heard through the open window the sound of chiming clocks and of bells ringing all over the city of Rome.

"One o'clock, there it is," Aunt Maria said. She hurried off to the kitchen from which came a delicious smell of cooking cheese and butter.

Italo went to the window and looked out. It was quite high up and he could see across the red-gold houses and the red-tiled roofs, the towers and domes of churches and other buildings. From the streets below came the sound of footsteps and voices, the creaking of carriages and the clop-clop of horses' hoofs. Over all was the brilliant midday sunshine.

Italo thought with tremendous excitement, "I'm in Rome!"

A small party of men in red shirts marched along the road. One of them, who seemed to be dressed no differently from the others, marched ahead of them. They were not in a straight line and they were not picking up their feet and putting them down in time like soldiers. As they marched they sang with great cheerfulness:

> "There were three hundred,
> Brave and strong.
> Now they are dead."

"What a sad song!" Italo said to Zelinda who had come to join him at the window.

"It is one of the songs of the Legion," Zelinda said. "I think it is sad. But Taddeo says not. He says it means that you do not fear death, that there are things worth dying for."

"All the same, I would much rather stay alive."

"So would Taddeo. There is a girl, Donata Bastini, with beautiful red hair, whom he wishes to marry. But he says that the freedom of Italy must come first."

Uncle Bibi and Taddeo came tramping upstairs. Aunt Maria came in from the kitchen, her face all smiles now, carrying a big earthenware dish heaped high with sizzling golden *gnocchi*. She put it down at one end of the table, which was spread with a beautiful white embroidered cloth. Taddeo heaped blue-black grapes and plump oranges on to another dish. They all stood up behind their chairs while Uncle Bibi said grace. Then, as Aunt Maria piled up the plates with *gnocchi*, Uncle Bibi uncorked the flask of wine that Italo had brought and filled their glasses.

"I will give you a toast," he said to them all. "Let us drink to the volunteer Red-Shirt, to Taddeo. May he distinguish himself in the battle and return to us in safety."

They all drank.

Taddeo cried out, "Thank you, thank you. But I must give you a toast now. To the Leader. To Garibaldi. To the heart and soul of the Italian people!"

"And now," Uncle Bibi said as they put down their glasses, "to Italo. Welcome to Rome, Italo."

They all drank, smiling at him and repeating, "Welcome to Rome, Italo."

Italo had another plateful of *gnocchi* and a lot of salad and some grapes and oranges, and began to feel very sleepy. It was only half a day since he had left his family and the farm, but it seemed like a whole day already. He was glad to think that it was now time for the siesta.

But first Taddeo had to go. Aunt Maria and Zelinda wept again, and Uncle Bibi had tears in his eyes. Italo felt like crying, too. Already he liked them all so much and did not want them to be unhappy. Also the sadness of the parting with Taddeo was mixed up with his own sadness that morning when he had said good-bye to his mother and father and Marco and Bernardo. Taddeo looked so much like Marco that it might have been Marco going off to the wars. Tears came into Italo's eyes, too. Taddeo was the only person who did not cry. He left them and they heard him tramping downstairs, and saw him in his red shirt swinging round the corner of the street.

"Now, Italo," Uncle Bibi said, "you must be tired. There is time for you to have a siesta before the shop opens."

He took Italo into Taddeo's room where a small bed had been made ready for him in one corner. The windows were shuttered and the room was cool. The dim light was very restful. Italo, as he lay down, put his hand into his shirt and felt the twig of cypress against his chest. It was one thing that seemed to be part of his old life and also of the new. In a minute, after he had laid his head down, he was fast asleep.

9

The English Artists

"There is no school today," Zelinda announced, skipping joyfully into the shop. "The nuns have sent us home because they are busy pushing all the furniture up against the doors and covering the windows with mattresses in case the French enter the city."

Uncle Bibi was weighing out a pound of onions for an old woman. When she had wrapped them up in a cotton handkerchief and taken them away, he turned round to Zelinda.

"Surely the Sisters do not think that the French would attack a Convent?"

"The Mother Superior says that when bullets and cannon balls are flying about in the streets no one can tell where they may go. So every opening must be stopped, and we have a holiday."

Zelinda picked up the skirts of her black school apron and spun round on the tips of her toes.

"Will there be fighting in this street?" Italo asked.

"I hope not," Uncle Bibi said seriously. "There won't unless the French overwhelm our army; Garibaldi has marched out to meet them on the Janiculum."

Zelinda stopped twirling and let her skirts fall. She had for the moment forgotten Taddeo.

"Let me help you in the shop, Papa," she begged.

"Stay and help me, then, while Italo takes their fruit to the English artists. It is quite easy to find the house, Italo. You go out of the square by the opposite corner and along the Via Barberina until you come to the third turning on the right. The house where they lodge, No. 4, is at the corner."

Italo and Zelinda watched while Uncle Bibi packed tomatoes, oranges, lemons and grapes into a big basket. Italo lifted it on to his shoulder and set off across the sunny square, where some little boys were splashing in the pool round the fountain.

"Give us an orange," they called out, but he shook his head and walked on past them.

He found the house, No. 4, at the corner of the third turning off the Via Barberina, and pulled the iron bell handle. There was no answer for a minute or two, then the door was opened by a woman with a baby in her arms.

"The English artists? They live on the third floor. You can leave the basket down here for them if you like. One of them is sure to be coming down."

"Thanks, I'll take it up," Italo said. After only two days in the shop he knew that it was just as well to get the money if he could when he delivered the orders.

He climbed up a steep narrow flight of stairs, reached the third floor and knocked on the door opposite to him.

"*Entra*," a voice called out. Italo pushed the door open, and stood looking round the room.

There were two young men there. One of them, who had a thatch of fair hair and a fair beard, was standing up in front of an easel with a paintbrush poised in his right hand and a palette smeared all over with different colors on his left thumb. The other young man, who was round and plump and dark, was half lying, half sitting on a couch looking through a portfolio of sketches.

The painter at the easel turned and saw Italo in the doorway with the basket of fruit on his shoulder.

"Oh, I say!" he exclaimed in English. "Hold it! Bill! Ask him to stand still."

The painter hastily snatched up a sheet of clean paper and slid it on to the easel.

Bill said to Italo in Italian, "Will you stand still for a few minutes? My friend, Roger, wants to make a sketch of you."

Puzzled, but interested, Italo began to lower the basket to the ground.

"No, no," Roger exclaimed. "Put it back! You'll ruin the whole thing! Bill . . ."

"My friend, who is too lazy to learn Italian, wants to paint you with the basket," Bill explained.

Italo put the basket back on his shoulder. He was pleased that the artist wanted to paint him, but the basket was heavy. He moved to take the weight more easily.

"Don't move," Roger shouted, drawing great lines on the paper with a piece of charcoal. "I'll pay you!"

Bill again translated.

"He wants you to stand perfectly still. Afterwards he will give you some money."

Italo kept as still as a stone boy on a fountain, except for his black eyes which were looking curiously round the room. It was very untidy and full of odd things. There was a heap of bright colored pieces of stuff, some of them almost rags, on one chair. On the table were a round loaf of bread, a knife, a lump of cheese, and a wicker-covered flask of wine. A lot of pictures without frames were propped against the walls. The sofa had been pushed into one corner, and on the end of it was a wide brimmed hat with a black plume in it, a sword in

54

an elaborate sheath, and a strip of bright green silk that trailed down on to the floor.

Roger made a last sweeping stroke with the piece of charcoal and stood back from the easel.

"Now tell him he can move," he said.

"My friend has finished his sketch," Bill said to Italo in Italian. "Come and look at it."

Italo thankfully put the heavy basket down on the floor and came to look, astonished that anybody could have drawn a picture so quickly.

He supposed that it was because the artist had drawn it in a hurry that he had no proper face in the picture. There was a black line for his cheek and another for his hair, and a sort of nose.

"It's only a first sketch," Bill explained. "He'll work it up afterwards. Perhaps he'll want you to come again. Would you be able to?"

"I'll ask my uncle. I work in his shop."

"Oh, yes, the fruit. Roger, have you got any money?"

Roger pulled open a drawer in a chest. It was full of socks and crumpled handkerchiefs, and letters and other things. He began to rummage about in it.

"I haven't seen you in your uncle's shop before," Bill said to Italo.

"No, I only came the day before yesterday."

"Then you are new to Rome. Come and look out of our window."

Italo looked out at an uneven sea of red tiles and high windows. Bill came to stand by him.

"Look over the roofs; there are the old walls of the city. That gate is the Porta San Pancrazio. Garibaldi and his men marched out that way to meet the French. There, that slope where you can see all those villas, is the Janiculum. They are fighting over the other side of it. Your people are on the crest of the hill and have the advantage of the ground. The French will have to attack up hill. I suppose the young man who generally works in the shop, wearing a red shirt, has gone to fight? Is he your cousin?"

"Yes. He is called Taddeo."

Roger had found some money. He paid for the fruit and gave Italo a few small coins for himself.

"Tell him," he said to Bill, "that I shall probably want him again. If I do I'll go along to the shop and ask his uncle when he can come."

Bill translated. Italo nodded. He hoped Uncle Bibi would let him come again. He had never seen any place like this before, nor spoken to any English people. It was all very interesting.

Roger pulled the sketch off the easel, and laid it flat on the table. Beneath it on the easel was a colored portrait of a man in a red shirt with reddish hair and beard, a broad open forehead and bright eyes.

"You know who that is?" Bill asked Italo.

Of course he knew. It was the face that appeared all over Italy in cheap, colored prints, on farmhouse walls and in village shops and in shop windows in Rome.

Italo said, "It's Garibaldi."

"Here's luck to him today!" Roger cried out. He went to the table and poured out two glasses of wine. "Let's drink his health!"

"Give the boy some, too," Bill said.

Roger filled a smaller glass and handed it to Italo.

"Garibaldi!" he said, lifting his glass up in the air. "May he send the French flying!"

He put down his empty glass and pointed to his picture. "How can they call that man a brigand, Bill? Look at his face. It is the face of a saint! One could use it for Christ in a holy picture."

"It is a noble head," Bill agreed. He asked Italo, "What is your name?"

"Italo."

"Italo the Italian. Remember, Italo, that we in England admire your Garibaldi so much that we could almost wish for his sake that we were Italians."

Roger picked up the sketch of Italo again and put it back on the easel. He took up the piece of charcoal and seized Italo by the arm, but Bill said, "Let the boy go now, Roger. You will get him into trouble. If you want him for a study, see his uncle about it."

Italo thought it was time to go, before Roger started making him stand still again. He bobbed his head to the two artists.

"Grazie, Signori. Thank you. Good morning."

He picked up the empty basket and scampered downstairs into the street.

10

Evviva Garibaldi!

"Italo, will you weigh out three pounds of potatoes, and a pound of small squash for the *Signora?*" Uncle Bibi said.

Italo began to tip potatoes into the scales.

"My son has just come back from the walls," the customer told them. "He says there was so much smoke from the firing over the Janiculum hill that it was impossible to see what was happening, but he met a wounded man hobbling back to the city who told him that our brave Roman boys, the students and the other volunteers, were in the advance guard, and the French attacked them first. Our poor lads were driven back; who could blame them when they had never heard a shot fired before? But Garibaldi sent the Legion in to support them, and himself led the volunteers back into the fight, and they drove the French down the hill again. But the French returned to the attack."

"Look after the shop for a moment, Italo," Uncle Bibi said when she had gone. He went upstairs to tell the news to his wife. A few minutes later she came down wearing a black lace veil over her hair. Zelinda, with a handkerchief tied over her head, came with her.

"We are going to the church," Aunt Maria said, "to light a candle for Taddeo and to pray for his safety."

58

Uncle Bibi put some money into Zelinda's hand.

"Buy a candle for me, too," he said, "and one for Italo."

"She loves Taddeo as her own son," he remarked as Aunt Maria and Zelinda turned the corner.

A minute or two later a man running down the street stopped to say breathlessly, "The French have fought their way to the top of the hill. They are occupying part of the Gardens of the Villa Corsini. It is said that Garibaldi is wounded, but is still on horseback leading the charges."

"Oh," Italo exclaimed in dismay, "Garibaldi wounded!"

"It may not be true." But Uncle Bibi frowned anxiously and weighed out so many tomatoes for a young woman who had asked for two pounds that they began to spill over the edge of her basket. She protested, "Do you want to rob yourself? I am not going to make tomato sauce for an army! Although I gladly would if only they all come safe home again. My brother-in-law is with the volunteers."

When she talked about making tomato sauce it reminded Italo of his mother and the kitchen at home. It was only three days since he had left the farm, but it seemed more like three months. What a long way off Pontevera and the quiet fields were from this crowded, noisy city with a battle going on outside the walls! For a minute Italo felt very homesick. He longed to be back playing with Anita or helping Marco and Bernardo to feed the beasts. He sat down on an upturned box, and rubbed his eyes so he would not cry.

"Would you like an orange for yourself, Italo?" Uncle Bibi handed him one that was slightly bruised. Italo felt better as he peeled the fruit and sucked the sweet juicy segments.

A customer came out of the barber's shop on the opposite side of the street. The barber, Renato, who was a friend of Uncle Bibi, strolled across to them wiping his hands on his striped apron.

"The *Signore* whom I have just shaved says that they are fighting in the rose gardens of the Corsini. When the smoke clears off a little you can see them from the walls. *Mamma mia!* If the French are on top of the hill our boys have lost the advantage of the ground. I should like to close the shop and go to the walls, but I cannot afford to lose customers. And my Gian Franco, who is not yet seventeen, is clamoring to put on a red shirt and join the volunteers! What times we live in! The young are all mad! You are fortunate that this nephew of yours is not yet old enough to fight."

"I belong to Young Italy," Italo said proudly. He was glad that in Rome he could boast about it; you did not have to make a secret of it as you did in the kingdom of Naples where the Strelli farm was.

Renato threw up his hands. "It is as I say: the young are all crazy. If you hear any news, Bibi, send the boy over to tell me."

Renato went back to his shop where another customer was waving impatiently to him from the doorstep.

About six o'clock Aunt Maria and Zelinda came from church. Zelinda, who had pulled the handkerchief off her head and was shaking out her hair, ran on ahead of her mother.

"Papa! Italo!" she cried out. "They are saying in the square outside the church that the French have been driven back towards the sea."

"It is true," Aunt Maria said, coming up more slowly. "There is talk of a victory, but how can you tell? One says this and one says that. Everyone comes back from the walls with a different story. I am going now to begin preparing supper."

"We will shut up the shop, Italo," Uncle Bibi said. "Everybody will be out in the streets waiting for news. I don't think we shall have any more customers this evening!"

They began to stack the boxes of fruit and vegetables and cover those that would keep till the next day. Italo was sweeping the floor of the shop and piling the scraps and rubbish into a basket, when suddenly he heard the sound of church bells. At first the sound came from St. Peter's, then from the middle of the city, then the bells of their own church in the next square began to ring. Soon the whole city of Rome seemed to be shaking with the sound of bells.

A boy running past shouted out, "A victory! The French have been driven back to the sea! A great victory for the Red-Shirts. *Evviva! Evviva! Evviva* Garibaldi!"

In a minute the street and the square were full of shouting people. They were waving flags, and singing and playing mouth organs. Some boys began to drag out old boxes and bits of paper to build a bonfire in the square. People running along the street shouted out news.

"They pushed the French right down the far side of the Janiculum! The French are making off as fast as they can to their ships at Civita Vecchia! Garibaldi was hit in the side by a bullet but is still on horseback, riding into the city. *Evviva! Evviva* the Red-Shirts! *Evviva* the Legion! *Evviva* the Bersaglieri! *Evviva* the Volunteers!"

Italo looked longingly at the boys making their bonfire.

"Go and join them, Italo," Uncle Bibi said, smiling.

"Let us all go!"

"It is no victory for us," Aunt Maria answered, "until we know that Taddeo is safe."

"Then I will wait, too." Italo resolutely turned his head away from the boys and the bonfire, and finished sweeping out the shop.

The bells were filling the air with their sound. Sometimes one church would be silent for a few minutes while the ringers had a rest, but there were always plenty of others still ringing. As dusk fell illuminations sprang up all over the city. People lit the gas in their houses and left their windows unshuttered and their curtains drawn back, so that the light streamed out into the streets. Fireworks went up into the sky, boys ran past carrying Bengal lights of emerald and blue and gold. The city rang with shouts of *"Evviva!"*

Uncle Bibi went restlessly to and fro between the doorway of his shop and the end of the street. Italo went with him, sometimes running off alone to look at the bonfire in the square. They tried to find out from everyone who came past whether the volunteers had marched back into the city, but they heard so many contradictory reports that it was impossible to tell what was really happening.

Italo strayed off for a minute to look at the bonfire. Suddenly he heard a great shout behind him. He turned and ran back. There, in the light from the shop doorway, stood Taddeo, his red shirt torn, his face blackened by powder but alive and safe. Italo and Zelinda danced round while Aunt Maria and Uncle Bibi embraced him and asked him questions so fast that he had no time to answer. All the people in the square, the boys round the bonfire, and the other people standing in their doorways, came running across to greet the volunteer home again. Taddeo laughed and waved his arms and tried to thank them and to tell them about the battle, but everybody was too much excited to listen.

"Wait a minute . . . a minute," Uncle Bibi shouted when all those who could reach Taddeo had embraced him and were turning away to go back to their own houses. Uncle Bibi dived into the shop and dragged out a big box full of oranges.

"Have some fruit," he shouted, "for your kindness in sharing our rejoicing." He took oranges out of the box and began to throw them to all the people in the square. Italo sprang to help him. It was a bombardment of golden balls. Some people caught theirs; others rolled and bounced on the ground, and the children scrambled for them.

"Our poor Taddeo is exhausted," Aunt Maria said. "Let us take him in to the house to eat."

They all went in except Italo, who was far too excited to be hungry. He picked up the empty orange box and ran joyfully to put it on the now dying bonfire. All the other boys ran back to it, and to the tune of mouth organs and bells they joined hands, Italo among them, and danced in a ring round and round the flames that leapt up from the dry wood of the box.

Their shrill voices rose above the crackle of wood and the squealing of the mouth organs.

"*Evviva!*" they shouted. "*Evviva* Garibaldi. *Evviva la Libertà! Evviva l'Italia!*"

Italo had never had such an exciting evening in his life.

Brothers Meet

"Stand still," Roger bellowed.

Bill, who generally translated for Roger, had gone out to buy some coffee, but now that Italo had been to their studio three or four times he knew those English words if he knew no others. He tried to stop fidgeting. It was a hot afternoon, the basket of fruit seemed particularly heavy today, and there was a tickle on his ankle which he very much wanted to scratch. It was dull, too, when Bill was not there since Italo and Roger could not talk much to one another.

"Now you can rest," Roger said. He waved a hand to try and show what he meant. Italo, who has beginning to know those words, too, thankfully lowered the basket of fruit to the ground and skipped to the window.

He loved looking out over the roofs of Rome from this high window. He could see right across over the walls and the road outside them to the rising slope of the Janiculum and the walls of the Corsini villa where Garibaldi had defeated the French three weeks ago. He could see all kinds of interesting things nearer at hand, little gardens up among the roofs where a few straggling plants grew in pots, and lines of washing waving like flags in a breeze. There was one high window where an old woman kept a bird in a cage outside, and another where a small black cat often sat washing himself on the window sill. In the short intervals that Roger allowed him Italo never grew tired of watching this roof-top world.

Roger was scratching away at something in the picture on his easel and frowning. When he was not actually painting Italo he never seemed to remember that he was in the room. Bill was much more friendly, and Italo was glad when he heard his footsteps coming up the stairs.

Bill came in with an armful of parcels, and an English *Times* newspaper. He threw them all down on the table.

"*Ciao,* Italo! Roof gazing as usual," he said pleasantly. He stepped across to look at the portrait on the easel, and patted Roger on the back. "It's coming on."

"The shadow under his chin is too heavy," Roger grumbled. "But I can't get it right today, somehow."

"Perhaps it's because you haven't had your coffee. I'll make some."

Roger lit the small oil stove, and put water on it to boil. He unwrapped a parcel, spooned some coffee beans into the brass mill and began to turn the handle to grind them.

"I'll do that," Italo said. He ground vigorously and sniffed the delicious smell of freshly milled coffee under his nostrils.

"I saw your Red-Shirt cousin was helping in the shop again yesterday," Bill said. "Isn't his name Taddeo? Doesn't he still belong to the volunteers?"

"Yes, but he sleeps at home, because the barracks are full. He goes nearly every day to exercises with the volunteers outside the walls. Sometimes there are no exercises, so he can help us in the shop."

"He won't have much time for the shop soon when the French come back. With more troops and big guns."

Italo looked surprised. "Are they coming back?"

"You're like everybody else in Rome, except Garibaldi. You think you've finished with them. Of course they're coming back. The French have a fine army, and are a great and proud nation. They have promised the Pope to restore him in Rome."

Bill pointed to the twig of cypress which Italo now wore pinned to his shirt.

"You won't be able to wear that so openly in a month or two perhaps. It will be a secret society again."

"It is now at home."

"What are you frowning at like that?" Bill asked.

"Because somebody told the secret at home and the soldiers came. Everybody thought I had told it because I was the youngest, but I hadn't."

"What a shame! Do you know who did give it away?"

"No. But I will find out some day when I go home again."

"I daresay you will. You're a bright boy. Have some coffee."

Roger threw his palette and his paintbrush across the room. "I can't do it today, my eye is out. Tell the boy he can go. Let's go and lie in the shade in the Borghese Gardens."

It was now near the end of May, and so hot outside that Italo was glad to walk on the shady side of the street. He came to be painted in the hour of the siesta because the shop was closed then and Uncle Bibi did not need him. Roger paid him a little money each time. Italo sometimes bought an ice cream on the way back to the shop, but he was saving up to buy a red shirt; also presents for his mother and for Anita that he could take next time he went home.

"Italo! Italo!"

Hearing somebody behind him calling his name he

turned round and to his astonishment saw Roberto from the mill and his cousin, Benito Lupini, both wearing red shirts.

"*Ciao,* Italo. *Ciao.*" Roberto laughed his great rumbling laugh. "You did not expect to see us here, did you?"

"No," Italo said coldly. He had not forgotten that morning at Enrico's in Pontevera, and how they had thought that he was the one who had betrayed Young Italy.

"Aha! You thought that you were the only one from Pontevera to come to Rome. But there are six of us here. We came yesterday to join the Red-Shirts. Your Marco, too."

"Marco here?" Italo suddenly realized how glad he would be to see his brother.

"Yes, there is only Bernardo on your farm now to help your father. And Lorenzo Crevi is here. Danielo stays to work on their farm." Roberto pointed to Italo's chest. "I see you still wear the twig of cypress."

"Why shouldn't I?" Italo asked fiercely. "It wasn't I who gave away the secret. It might just as well have been you."

Roberto laughed as he laughed at everything, but Benito said smoothly, "Anyhow, that is all over and forgotten now."

"I don't forget," Italo muttered. "Where is Marco?"

"Somewhere in Rome. We all signed on with the volunteers this morning. Now since the houses they are using for barracks are full we have to find somewhere to sleep. Perhaps your uncle . . ."

"No, there is no room."

"Oh, well, we had better be looking about."

"I must go back to the shop," Italo said. "It will be opening again. *Ciao,* Roberto. *Ciao,* Benito."

67

"*Ciao,* Italo."

They went on along the pavement. Italo heard a church clock strike three and began to run. Taddeo was exercising with the volunteers today and Uncle Bibi would be in the shop alone.

But he was not. As he turned the corner Italo saw a tall lithe figure in a red shirt by Uncle Bibi's side in the shop doorway. He thought that the exercises must have finished in the morning and Taddeo must have come back. He slowed down, wiping the sweat off his face with his sleeve. Then he saw that it was not Taddeo who stood by Uncle Bibi; he had been deceived in the distance by the family likeness. It was Marco! Italo shot forward as if he had been a stone shot out of his own catapult, and sprang into Marco's ready arms, overjoyed to see his own brother from home.

12

The Picnic

"This is the happiest day of my life!" Zelinda cried. She rolled over luxuriously on the dry grass. She and Italo and Marco and Taddeo were eating an *al fresco* meal, a picnic in the Borghese Gardens on the hillside above Rome. It was June 1st, and the shop was shut because the Triumvirs had declared a public holiday to celebrate the treaty which they had signed the day before with De Lesseps, the French Envoy.

"Now you won't have to fight any more," Zelinda said. De Lesseps had promised that the French would keep their troops outside Rome, and would protect the city, if necessary, against Austria and Naples.

"Oh, yes, we shall," Marco answered her. "Now that Rome is safe, Garibaldi will lead us north to drive the Austrians out of Milan and Venice."

Zelinda looked disappointed.

"I thought it was all over. The bells were ringing last night again and we had fireworks."

"Only part of the battle is over. We shall never stop fighting until the whole of Italy is one free nation. We shall all march north very soon."

"Will you have to go too, Taddeo?"

"Of course. Papa has agreed that I should go with the volunteers wherever Garibaldi leads them."

"But you won't go, Italo?"

"I wish I could," Italo answered. "I shall be thirteen in three months."

"No, no, Italo. You must stay and help Papa with the shop or I could not go." Taddeo, who had his guitar across his knees, began to play the song of the legion:

> "There were three young men
> Strong and brave.
> Now they are dead."

"Oh, please, Taddeo, don't play that sad tune."

Taddeo smiled.

"Very well. I will play a dance tune."

He began to play the Marseillaise, the French National Anthem, in dance time. People in Rome had been doing this to show that they were not afraid of the French. It was a way of making fun of them.

"You mustn't play that now," Marco said. "Since yesterday the French are our allies and protectors. It is not right any more to mock their song."

Taddeo stopped playing it. He always obeyed and followed Marco, who was just as much the one who gave orders to the younger part of the family here as he had been on the Strelli farm.

"Marco is quite right," Zelinda said seriously. She gazed at him with admiration. She thought her cousin Marco the handsomest and most exciting person she had even seen.

"Play a marching song," Italo suggested.

Taddeo struck up a spirited tune.

"Everybody is up here today making holiday," Zelinda murmured happily. She looked round at the many little groups scattered about on the grass.

A voice said in English, "Why, it's Italo." He looked

up and saw Roger and Bill strolling along the path, both smoking thin Italian cigars. Roger had his sketchbook under his arm. He looked at the group on the grass with his eyes screwed up in the way in which he sometimes looked at Italo when he was painting his picture of him.

Then he said something to Bill in English.

Bill translated into Italian. "My friend would very much like to sketch you all if you wouldn't mind. Just a quick sketch. If you could keep still only for five minutes?"

Zelinda, delighted, sat up and began to smooth her hair and straighten her dress.

"No, no!" Roger said.

"He wants you all just as you are," Bill explained. "You, my friend, go on playing your guitar. You, Zelinda, isn't it?—you are pretty as you are just like that with your hair falling about."

Roger sat down on a hummock. Bill squatted on the grass near them. Italo rolled an orange towards him. Bill nodded his thanks and began to peel it and suck the juicy segments.

Taddeo went on gently plucking at his guitar and humming to himself. The other three stiffened into unnatural attitudes. Roger made an impatient gesture, and uttered an exclamation.

"Forget about Roger drawing you," Bill said. "He can do it much better if you are not thinking about him. I suppose the shop is shut as you are all here."

"Yes, for the peace holiday."

"Ah, the peace holiday," Bill said thoughtfully. "Rome is very trustful."

Roger, drawing furiously in his sketchbook, said in English, "Don't spoil it for them, Bill. Let them enjoy it while they can."

71

"Yes, I agree," Bill replied, also in English. He went on, in Italian, "This morning, Italo, the little black cat that you always watch from our window came across the roofs to visit us, and I put out some milk for him in a saucer on the window sill. When he had drunk every drop he mewed to me to thank me, and then he was off over the roofs again. They are so hot now at midday that he cannot walk on them except in the shade of a chimney pot. I see him put out his paw on to the sunny tiles and then quickly draw it back again."

"Poverino," Italo said, smiling.

"Oh, he is very happy, he has a good home. If he is away for too long his old mistress looks so anxiously out of the window and calls to him, and he comes skipping back to her across the tiles with his tail up as if it were the mast of a small ship."

"That will do." Roger tore the sheet off his block, and smiled for the first time. *"Mille grazie,"* he said carefully. He had learned how to thank people in Italian.

"Please show me," Zelinda begged.

She found the picture rather disappointing, as Italo had done when he first saw his. All that she could see of herself was a few black lines, an arm, a leg, a shoulder, a hanging piece of hair, the side of a cheek.

"He hasn't drawn my face," she complained.

"Come on, Roger," Bill said in English. "Draw the lady's face for her. You can't expect everything for nothing."

Roger shrugged his shoulders, but he opened his sketchbook again and sat for a minute or two looking intently at Zelinda. Then he drew rapidly, while she held her breath.

Roger tore the sheet off his sketchbook and handed it to her with a little bow. It was still only a few black

72

lines, but this time he had drawn the whole of her face with her two eyes wide open and her nose and her full lips, and the hair falling on either side of it.

Zelinda showed it to Marco who smiled and said, "*Bella, bella!*"

Zelinda breathed a sigh of pleasure. "I said this was my happiest day."

"Keep that," Bill told her. "One day Roger will be a famous artist, and everyone will want to see that. You will be able to sell it for a lot of money."

"I shall never, never sell it." Zelinda clutched it to her chest.

"That's the spirit." Bill laughed.

Taddeo offered the two Englishmen the big wicker-covered flask of wine. They both drank, and Bill said, "*Saluti. Alla Libertà! All' Italia!*"

"*Saluti,*" Roger echoed, tipping the wine down his throat.

The artists said good-bye and walked on. Italo rolled over on to his stomach and looked down at the roof tops of Rome below. He wished he had a telescope, one of the things he had learnt about since he came to Rome. If he had one he might be able to see the little black cat asleep in the shade of a chimney pot.

"*Ciao,* Marco! *Ciao,* Taddeo! *Ciao,* Zelinda! *Ciao,* Italo!"

Italo rolled over and sat up. Roberto and Benito were standing above the group. They, too, were smoking cigars, and their twigs of cypress were pinned on to their red shirts. Italo rolled over again on his face. Nothing, nothing would ever make him like Benito and Roberto who had suspected him of treachery. He was annoyed because Marco and Taddeo said, "*Ciao,*" to them in quite a friendly way, and Zelinda, who was getting above herself, looked up at them from under her eyelashes.

"What fine news this is," Benito said. "How wonderful that Rome is safe, and will be protected by the French!"

"Yes, we were right to come here," Roberto agreed. Italo, lying on his face, heard his silly laugh. "We were clever, Marco, you and I and Benito, we came just after the battle was over."

"I would rather have been here to fight," Marco said fiercely.

"No, no, it is much better now, eh, Benito?"

Benito said smoothly, "We must all honor and envy Taddeo, who did fight in the defense of Rome."

Italo muttered to himself, "He doesn't mean it." He snorted and rubbed his nose in the dry, hot grass, wishing that he could rub Benito's.

"We *shall* fight," Marco cried. "We shall march to free the rest of Italy."

"My mother in the country has only me," Benito said. "I cannot go too far away from her."

"We all have mothers," Marco replied.

Taddeo began to play his guitar again and softly sang a verse of a Neapolitan love song.

"That is it," Roberto giggled. "Tonight there will be more illuminations and more fireworks and we will all dance in the streets and make love."

Italo sat up and said, "If you can find a girl who will have you."

He meant that to be insulting, but Roberto thought it was very funny, and let out his loud guffaw. Italo lay down again. It was simply not worth while being rude to a fool like Roberto.

Taddeo again offered the flask of wine. Roberto and Benito drank, and with a few more words walked on.

Italo did not sit up to call out *"Ciao,"* to them. He went on lying with his face in the grass.

Taddeo, who felt something wrong, asked, "Are you asleep, Italo?"

"No."

"Are you thirsty? There is still a little wine left, I think."

"I do not drink after Benito," Italo answered.

Suddenly saying something that he had not known he thought, he cried out, "I believe it was he who betrayed us at Pontevera. That fool Roberto blabbed to him."

Taddeo said, "But Benito belongs to Young Italy. He is wearing the twig of cypress."

"Yes, now, here, where it is safe to wear it."

Marco said thoughtfully, "We shall never know."

"I shall know," Italo replied. "Somehow I shall find out."

Taddeo said gently, "We must not say what we do not know of one of our brothers in Young Italy."

He began to sing and play again as if he wanted to put an end to the talk. He played softly and soon the others were all asleep lying round him on the warm grass. It was evening before they left the Borghese Gardens, and began with all the other groups of holiday makers to walk along the Pincian Hill and down the long flight of Spanish Steps into Rome.

There were a great many people standing talking at the street corners and in the doorways of cafés and wine shops, but this was usual in the evening. Italo and the others were content and a little dazed, with their long day in the fresh air on the higher ground. They were also hungry. It seemed many hours since their picnic lunch. "I know what we are going to have for supper," Zelinda told them. "Mamma bought two rabbits late last night and put them to stew with wine and herbs

75

early this morning." Zelinda walked with little skips. To have Marco and Italo living with them made it seem as if they were having a party every evening.

Suddenly above their heads and all round them the church bells of Rome began to ring.

"Are they ringing again for the peace?" Zelinda asked. "They did that last night."

A man wearing a red shirt ran past them, carrying his musket. He called out to them. "It is the alarm."

"Diamine!" Marco exclaimed. "What can it be?"

"It could only be the Neapolitans marching on us before the French are here to protect us," Taddeo replied.

Both he and Marco began to run. Italo and Zelinda, who had no idea what was happening, ran after them. All four turned into the street where the shop was, and, as they came near, saw Uncle Bibi on the pavement outside the shop door watching for them.

"There is bad news," he said as they ran up to him. "The treaty was a trick. De Lesseps has cheated us. The French have landed at the port of Civita Vecchia with thirty thousand men and six batteries of artillery. Marco, Taddeo, you are summoned at once to your headquarters. The French are marching on Rome!"

13

After the Battle

"It is another holiday today," Zelinda said, "because the sisters are putting all the mattresses back again at the windows. But the French won't come, will they? The Red-Shirts will beat them again, won't they?"

"Don't stand there chattering," Uncle Bibi said sharply. "You get in Italo's way when he is putting out the boxes. Run upstairs to your mother."

Uncle Bibi hardly ever spoke sharply to Zelinda, and Italo knew that it was because he was worried. Zelinda disappeared. Italo went on arranging the boxes of fruit and vegetables so that customers could see them.

Uncle Bibi pushed back the bead curtain that covered the doorway and went outside. Italo saw him leaning against the doorpost and wiping the sweat off his bald head.

A customer came out of the barber's shop opposite. Renato walked across to join Uncle Bibi. Renato, too, looked anxious.

"I have decided to shut the shop at noon," he said. "Anyone who has not come before then must wear a beard till tomorrow. I cannot bear another day of waiting for rumors from the battlefield. I shall go and watch from the walls. Do you know that my Gian Franco has run off without a word? His mother says he must have gone to volunteer, but I pray to the Madonna that he has only gone to the walls. They say the French have far more men this time and big guns."

Italo longed to go and watch from the walls, too, but when he suggested it Uncle Bibi only shook his head.

"It is better to keep on working," he said. "When one is anxious it passes the time."

They did not have many customers in the first part of the morning. Those who came were hurried and anxious.

"It is not worth while buying much," one woman said. "After all, who knows what will happen? Perhaps the French will come before nightfall, and if so my old man says that we will load as much as we can on to a cart, and go to my brother's farm near Tivoli until we see how things are here." She added, "There are so many of the French this time and they have big guns."

"It does not do to expect the worst," Uncle Bibi said to her.

When she had gone he turned to Italo. "Now, while things are quiet, you had better take their salad and fruit to your English friends."

Italo by now knew exactly what Bill and Roger liked and could fill the basket for them himself. He hoisted it on to his shoulder and started off, pleased as always to get out into the streets and see what was going on.

There were not many men about. Most of those who could get off work had gone to the walls to try and see something of the fighting on the Janiculum. The women were standing in the doorways of their houses calling to each other any bit of news that came from a passer-by. Italo reached the house in the Via Barberina, and climbed the steep stairs.

At first when he knocked at the door of the artists' apartment there was no answer, and he thought that there was no one in. He knocked again and heard Bill shout, *"Entra."*

When Italo pushed the door open and went in, he saw that Roger and Bill were both leaning out of the open window, and Roger was looking through a pair of binoculars.

Bill drew in his head.

"Ah, there you are, Italo. Put the vegetables in that corner out of the sun, will you?" He added, "We are watching the battle. We can see quite clearly through these glasses. Do you want to have a look?"

"Yes! Yes, thank you!"

Italo came forward eagerly to the window. Roger did not at once give up the glasses. Italo peered out over the red-tiled roofs, with their festoons of washing hanging here and there from window to window, over the walls of Rome to the green hillside dotted with villas. He could see clouds of smoke and dust, tiny figures in red and blue moving, a flag waving.

"Let Italo have a look, Roger," Bill said. "After all, it's his war."

Roger handed over the glasses. At first Italo could only see two circles with blurred pictures in them, in which green branches seemed to be waving against the deep blue sky.

"Move that up and down until you can only see one circle," Bill said.

Italo adjusted the glasses until the two circles ran into one. Now he could see quite clearly, as if he was close to it, a rose garden and a path running uphill through it. Sometimes smoke and dust blew across so that the path was hidden, then it cleared and he saw figures in red shirts advancing up the path, with their bayonets at the ready. Then one fell and rolled over on to a flower bed; another stumbled to his knee. Other figures came for-

79

ward into the circle: a Red-Shirt carrying a banner, a Montevidean tiger recognizable by his long hair.

"The French stole a march on your people," Bill said. "They occupied the Villa Corsini very early this morning. Now the Red-Shirts are trying to drive them out. But the French are sheltered by the walls of the villa, and they have been firing from behind the box hedges and the tubs of orange trees. All the same, the Italian Legion have nearly forced an entrance twice. I saw Garibaldi quite clearly fighting on the steps of the villa with his white South American poncho swirling around him. It is strange to wear that heavy cloak in battle in the summer, but no doubt it keeps the bullets off."

Italo had never looked through binoculars before. It seemed to him so wonderful to be able to see things so far off as if they were near to him. He almost forgot for a moment that it was a real battle that he was watching and that Marco and Taddeo must be somewhere in the fight. Then as he shifted the binoculars he saw a young man in a red shirt lying doubled up across a rose-bed, and suddenly he could not look any more. He handed the binoculars back to Roger, who clapped them to his eyes again.

"They're in," he said. "I saw the flag of the Legion go in at the doorway of the villa. But they'll never stay there. They're brave enough, but they don't know the game and the French do. What chance has a mob against an army?"

"Garibaldi beat the French last time," Italo said fiercely.

"Yes, but there weren't so many of them and they didn't really expect much fighting. This time they've taken him seriously."

"I must go back to the shop now," Italo said. He felt that he did not want to stay any longer with Roger, who was watching the battle as if it was a game, because he belonged to another country. Italo would rather be with Uncle Bibi who was an Italian like himself, to whom it mattered. Bill seemed to understand this; he put a hand on Italo's shoulder.

"You know we are on your side, the side of the Red-Shirts. You must not think we do not care."

When Italo came in sight of the shop again he saw that a man in a red shirt was standing in the doorway talking to Uncle Bibi. Italo sprang forward. Marco? Taddeo? Then, as he came nearer, he saw that it was neither of them. It was Benito Lupini. Not even a red shirt, Italo thought, could make Benito look anything but mean and ugly, with his pale face and his long nose and his two little eyes that looked as if they were trying to see one another across it. And why wasn't Benito fighting with the others? Italo scowled at him.

Benito always tried to be very friendly to Italo, as if he knew that Italo didn't like him and wanted to make him friendly, too.

"*Ciao*, Italo," he called out, waving to him. "You will be surprised to see me here today. But since I am used to working in an office and keeping accounts they have made me one of the storekeepers at the barracks. You can imagine how much I wish I was out there with the others, driving off the French. I longed to go with Marco and Taddeo. But someone has to see that there is food and bedding for our brave lads when they come back from the battlefield." He turned again to Uncle Bibi.

"So you will let us have ten cases of tomatoes and ten cases of oranges? I will send a cart for them, and again the day after tomorrow. You will be well paid. If I do not call myself, one of the other storekeepers will come and settle your account. You will give us discount, of course, because we are taking large quantities?"

"I would give you discount anyhow," Uncle Bibi replied, "since it is for the Red-Shirts."

"That is right," Benito said. "You are a good patriot."

Italo thought that Benito sounded dreadfully patronizing and made a face at him behind his back.

Benito said, "*Ciao,* Signor Fantoni, *ciao,* Italo," and walked off.

Uncle Bibi said, "It is through your family, Italo, that this large order has come to me. A thousand thanks."

Italo scowled. "I hate Benito."

"Oh? Why?"

"I just hate him."

Somehow Italo did not feel able to tell Uncle Bibi, as he had told the younger ones, that he suspected Benito of having betrayed Young Italy at Pontevera and blamed him, Italo, for it.

At the moment, Uncle Bibi was so much worried about the battle, and about Taddeo and Marco, that he was not really attending to what Italo was saying. He only answered, "I shall shut up half an hour before the time and we will go to the church and say a prayer for those who are fighting."

The church was already full of people praying. There were women with black lace scarves or handkerchiefs over their heads, men who had slipped in for a few minutes from their offices or shops. Uncle Bibi bought two candles from the old man selling them at the door and handed one to Italo. They lit the candles and placed them in the stand in front of the statue of the Madonna with the baby Christ in her arms. Aunt Maria and Zelinda were already kneeling there. Zelinda had covered her face with her hands, but she saw Italo from between her fingers and just moved one hand for a minute and smiled at him. She made a sign to him to come and kneel beside her.

It was very cool and quiet in the church, which smelled of incense and old stone. Italo, through his half-shut eyes, watched the pointed flames of the candles burning upwards against the Madonna's blue robe. He shut his eyes more tightly and prayed hard for Marco and Taddeo.

As they were going home they saw a big man in a red shirt coming along the street.

"It's Roberto," Italo cried. "Roberto from the mill. The battle must be over. Roberto," Italo shouted across the street, "what is happening? Have we won? Where are the others?"

Roberto came across the street to them. His red shirt had one sleeve torn half off; his hair was ruffled up on top of his head; he looked quite pale, and frightened.

"I do not like fighting," he said. "My father told me not to come and he was right. I am going home, now, to Pontevera."

"Is the battle over?"

"No, it is still going on. It is terrible. The French are devils. You cannot see where they are, and then suddenly they shoot from behind a hedge. They are hidden behind every bush in the Corsini garden. My father said I shouldn't like it and he was quite right. I am going back to the mill."

"Taddeo?" they shouted at him. "Marco? Are they all right? Have you seen them?"

"I have not seen Taddeo since we advanced up the hill. There is so much smoke and noise it is very hard to see anyone. But, yes, I did see Marco just before I came away. The French took our flag and were carrying it off when Marco ran forward into the middle of them and came back carrying the flag. There were bullets flying all round him, and all our Red-Shirts cheered."

"Was he hurt? Was he safe?"

"No, he was not hurt, but the flag was full of bullet holes. It was a miracle that they did not hit Marco. I do not think it was worth while," Roberto shook his head, "to take that risk just for a flag! The flag was spoilt, anyhow, full of holes and all black with powder. I would have let the French have it. Afterwards we could have got a new one for ourselves."

"Marco would not think so," Italo said proudly.

"Well, I think so. Let the French have as many flags as they like. I do not care about fighting." And Roberto added, "I do not want to wear the twig of cypress any more." He pulled roughly at the twig of cypress which was pinned on his shirt and threw it down on the dusty pavement. "I have finished with all that," he said. "I do not care if Mazzini and Garibaldi or the Pope rule in Rome. I do not like Rome. It is too big and there is too much noise. I am going back today to the mill at Pontevera. *Addio! Addio!*"

He shambled off along the street before they could ask him any more questions.

"He will not be much loss to the Red-Shirts," Uncle Bibi remarked.

"No," Aunt Maria agreed, "so long as there are not many more like him who do the same."

"Anyhow, Marco is not like him," Uncle Bibi said to Italo. "We can be proud of him. He is evidently proving himself a gallant soldier." He added to Aunt Maria, "That this fool has not seen Taddeo is nothing. As he says, it would be difficult to see clearly in the smoke and confusion, and our friend Roberto would be thinking only of himself and saving his own skin."

They were all very silent at lunch. Only Italo and Zelinda could eat large platefuls of the spaghetti which Aunt Maria ladled out of the smoking pan.

All through the long summer afternoon, people came back from the walls with anxious faces.

"Garibaldi and the Legion have charged again and again but they cannot drive the French out of the Villa Corsini."

"Our poor lads are mown down by the fire from the French rifles as they advance up the garden paths."

"You can see the fallen Red-Shirts lying in the garden like fallen petals of red roses."

"Let us go to the walls, Uncle Bibi," Italo entreated.

"No, we must keep together. There may be great confusion in Rome later."

Uncle Bibi did not say: "If the French come," but Italo knew what he was thinking. Perhaps, after all, the nuns had been wise to put their mattresses up against the windows of the convent.

As the sun began to set, people came past with white faces.

"The Red-Shirts are in retreat. The French have driven them off the Janiculum. Heaven help us all!"

"May I go to the Englishmen's apartment?" Italo begged. "I can see from their window what is happening. They will let me look through their binoculars. I will only run there and look and come back again."

Uncle Bibi hesitated.

"Well, run, then, and stay only a minute or two and come straight back."

Italo ran through the streets where every doorway was now filled with distracted people. Many of the women were weeping. Italo reached the house in the Via Barberina, and found the front door open. He climbed the stairs and knocked on his friends' door. There was no answer. Italo knocked again, then tried the handle but the door was locked. Perhaps Roger and Bill had gone to the walls or out to a café as they often went in the evening. Italo ran downstairs again and raced home, pushing his way through the crowds of men standing outside the cafés.

He found the shop shut. Zelinda was sitting forlornly on the doorstep at the side entrance. Italo sat down by her. In the square, where they had lit the joyful bonfire a few weeks ago, the boys were scuffling in a half-hearted way round the fountain. The older people were standing about talking to one another. Every now and then they stopped to listen as if they expected either to hear their own Red-Shirts coming home or the French entering the city.

"Mamma is crying upstairs," Zelinda said. "And Papa is with her. How horrid it all is now! What shall we do if the French come?" She began to cry herself.

Italo put an arm round her.

"I shall look after you if the French come. Perhaps I will take you away from Rome to our farm at Pontevera. Do you remember the farm? You could stay there safe with Mamma and my father until the French have gone away again."

He began to talk softly about the farm as they sat on the step in the warm summer darkness.

"We have such a lot of olive trees. It takes us all several weeks to pick the olives in the autumn. And we have beautiful vines; we planted some new ones three years ago. And we have two white oxen, Nello and Buffo; and we have milk cows, and hens that lay fine brown eggs, and such a lot of rabbits. You would like to see the rabbits with their long furry ears and their bright eyes. And you could help me to find the eggs; there is one silly hen who always hides hers and I have to look for them . . ."

Italo went on telling her about the farm, partly to

86

comfort her, partly to comfort himself. After a time he felt her head fall against his shoulder, and heard her gentle breathing as she slept. Italo, too, grew sleepy, and instead of talking about the farm he slipped into a dream about it. He thought he was back in the long bedroom under the roof at home, so that it seemed like part of the dream when he heard Marco's voice above him.

"Where is Uncle Bibi?"

Italo half woke up. Zelinda stirred on his shoulder.

"Upstairs," Italo said.

"Let me past." Marco pushed past Italo and tramped upstairs. Still only half awake Italo began to remember where he was and what had been happening. He gently pushed Zelinda away from him so that she slept on, leaning against the door post. Italo followed Marco upstairs, stumbling a little from sleepiness and rubbing his eyes.

In the room over the shop the gas was lit, and Uncle Bibi and Aunt Maria, sitting near the open window, looked round with startled faces at Marco in the doorway. As the sleep cleared from his eyes Italo saw that Marco's face was black with powder and he had a bandage round his arm. He held on to the back of a chair as if utterly exhausted.

"Taddeo?" Uncle Bibi asked.

Marco tried to speak, swallowed, and then said in a low, hoarse voice, "It was this evening when we were being driven back down the hill from the Corsini. A wounded man on the ground called out to us to help him and we went back for him. There was a Frenchman behind a box hedge. He shot Taddeo through the heart."

14

Roof-top View

"Where have you been, Italo?" Bill asked. "You haven't brought us our salad for three days. You look rather peaky. Have you been ill?"

"The shop was shut," Italo explained, "because my cousin, Taddeo, was killed in the battle."

"I'm sorry. I'm very sorry." Bill put a hand on Italo's shoulder, and spoke to Roger in English. Roger, who was mixing paints, laid down his palette and came across the room.

"I'm sorry, too," he said. He was very slowly learning how to speak some Italian, but he was not a person who said much in any language. Italo knew by now that Bill was the friendly one, but that Roger meant to be friendly only he didn't always know how.

Roger went back to his paints.

"Please tell your poor uncle how sorry we both are," Bill said. "I shall come and see him. Don't go for a minute, Italo. I went out and bought some strawberries because I didn't know whether you'd be coming. I see you've brought some more, so you must eat mine. And you must have a look out of the window at your little black cat and see how he's getting on. You haven't seen him for days."

Italo felt that it was such a relief to be in a place

where people were cheerful and ordinary again. Uncle Bibi had not laughed his jolly laugh since the news about Taddeo had come. Aunt Maria and Zelinda cried all the time, and Marco, when he was not on duty with the volunteers, was stern and silent. Here with his English friends Italo felt better. He gobbled up a large plateful of strawberries, and then went to kneel on the window sill and look out across the roof-top world.

"Oh," he exclaimed. "What is that? What has happened on the Janiculum? Up there in front of the Villa Corsini?"

All along the edge of the green hill where the battle had raged there was a great mound of freshly dug earth stretching right across the front of the Corsini garden, and far beyond it.

"Those are the French earthworks," Bill said. "They dug themselves in all night after the battle. When we looked out of the window in the morning we saw that mound."

"What is it for?"

"To protect them from another attack, and probably to act as a screen while they bring up their siege guns and make emplacements for them. But I don't think they will fire on Rome if they can help it. They won't want to destroy the Holy City. All they want is to turn out Mazzini and the Triumvirs and put the Pope back. They hope Mazzini will surrender."

"He won't, will he?"

Bill looked doubtful.

"I don't see what else he can do in the end. The French General Oudinot has brought a large well-equipped force. I am afraid, my little twig of cypress, that it will be some time yet before you see your free and united Italy. But you will see it, I think, in your lifetime."

"Does it say so in the English *Times* newspaper?" Italo asked solemnly.

"Not yet, but one day you will read about it there. I hope I shall be in Rome, and you and I will go out and celebrate together."

"And light a bonfire?" Italo asked eagerly. "And have fireworks?"

"Oh, certainly, light a bonfire and have fireworks. Look," Bill pointed across the rooftops. "That tall house with the tower and the flag flying on it is the Villa Savorelli, where Garibaldi has made his headquarters. It is right up against the wall of Rome. From the balcony on the other side Garibaldi can see the French camp and watch their movements. The French keep on firing at the Savorelli and knocking bits off it. It is about as far as the guns they have there now will reach. And they say there are snipers in the no-man's land between the French and Rome always ready to try and pick off the General when he comes out on to the balcony. If Garibaldi was out of the way, there would be no more fighting. Mazzini might want to defend Rome but he could not make the others do it alone."

Roger had stopped mixing his paints and begun to touch up his picture. It was a picture of a woman sitting sewing on the doorstep of her house. Italo came and stood behind Roger to watch. The wall of the house was the color of an apricot, the woman had a red shawl over her shoulders. Her white sewing fell in a cascade over her black skirt. Italo thought that if he could paint he would paint soldiers in uniform and generals and Red-Shirts and horses. An old woman sitting in a doorway was a thing you could see anywhere every day. Bill said to him, "It's beautiful, isn't it, Italo? Look at the shadow on that stone."

"Yes, beautiful," Italo said politely.

Roger spoke to Bill in English. Bill picked up Roger's portfolio of sketches and pulled out the sketch of the picnic party in the Borghese Gardens on the holiday. Taddeo was in the foreground of the picture, bending over his guitar.

"Roger wants you to give this to your uncle," Bill said. "Perhaps it will make him sad now, but he may like to keep it. Come tomorrow and bring us our salad and some strawberries if your uncle has any."

When Italo got back to the shop he found Uncle Bibi filling a large basket with fresh green lettuces and new young peas, and strawberries and cherries.

"Italo," he said, "will you go now to the Villa Savorelli, where Garibaldi has made his headquarters. We are very fortunate. Marco has been appointed one of the General's orderlies, and has given our name to the officer in charge of the mess. We shall supply vegetables and fruit to the Villa every day if the cooks are satisfied with the quality."

Italo handed over the sketch. "Roger sent this for you."

Uncle Bibi looked at it quickly, and tears came into his eyes. He put the sketch carefully on the table where he added up the accounts.

"It is very kind of your friend. I shall thank him. Now, Italo, if you do not see your way to the side entrance you must ask the sentry on duty by the front door. Ask the cook to let us know if there is anything the General specially likes, and we will get it for him if it can be got. Go as fast as you can and keep in the shade so that the lettuces arrive cool and fresh. When you come back it will be time for lunch."

Italo hoisted the basket on to his shoulder and set off in the direction of the Villa Savorelli.

29039 Charlotte County Free Library
Charlotte Court House, Va.

15

The Villa Savorelli

"Where is the Villa Savorelli?" Italo called out to another errand boy with an empty basket who was coming towards him along the cobbled street.

The boy jerked his head backwards. "Where I've just come from. When you turn the corner you'll see it, a great big house with a tower. But you take my advice and don't go there."

"Why not?" Italo asked.

"Because it's not safe. The French are shooting at it all the time. While I was going round to the side entrance a great lump of stone off one of the walls nearly fell on my head. I'm not going again, for anybody, not if I get sacked. Let the Red-Shirts come and fetch their own pies for dinner. You take my tip and turn back."

"My brother's a Red-Shirt," Italo said. "And I've taken the twig of cypress. I'm going on."

"Suit yourself," the other boy said. He swung his basket to and fro, and vanished, whistling.

Italo went on. As the boy had said, when he turned the next corner he saw the big villa like a palace, that must be the Villa Savorelli. He knew it must be, because there were so many Red-Shirts and other people going in and out of the great front doors, where two of the Tigers of Montevideo, with their long hair and broad-brimmed hats, stood on guard. Italo saw that the flag of the *Risorgimento*, the Italian colors of red, white and green with the words "Liberty, Equality, Humanity" printed across the stripes, was flying from the top of the tower. Was it a good thing, Italo wondered, to show the French where Garibaldi's headquarters were so that they could keep on shooting at it? But of course Garibaldi was never afraid of anything, and Italo wished to be like him. All the same, he hoped no piece of the wall would drop on him as he was looking for the side door.

He stopped for a minute to watch the soldiers and the other people in ordinary dress who kept on appearing in the main doorway, or disappearing through it. Then he remembered that the strawberries and lettuces would be wilting in the heat. He walked across the front of the villa and turned down a narrow street at the side.

There were several side entrances to the villa, but he could tell which was the kitchen entrance by the delicious smells of roasting meat and savory sauce that came floating out on to the summer air. He pushed his way in with his basket, past two or three kitchen boys who were scuffling about in the doorway.

He found himself in a long room with big fires blazing at one end. There were several cooks in white caps and coats busy over the fires. Every minute or so one of them would stop and wipe the sweat off his forehead with his sleeve, as Italo had seen his mother do on hot days in the kitchen at home. He lowered the basket from his shoulder and hoisted it on to one end of a long table. One of the cooks came bustling across to him.

"Now then, what have you got there? What shop do you come from?"

"This is the General's salad, and fruit, from Riccardo Fantoni."

"Empty your basket, then, on to that tray, and let me see it."

Italo lifted out the fresh green lettuces with the sprinkled drops of water on them like dew drops, and the panniers of strawberries. The cook inspected the lettuces, and tasted a strawberry. He nodded.

"Yes, your stuff is fresh, and these strawberries have been well washed. You can bring the same tomorrow, and three dozen lemons."

"My uncle told me to ask if there was anything that the General specially liked, so that he could be sure to get it when the carts come in to the market in the early morning."

The cook threw up his hands. "The General! If you gave him a slice of bread and a pitcher of water he would be perfectly satisfied. In fact, that is his supper most nights when he's fighting or travelling. I was with the Legion in Montevideo, you see. I know his ways. But we give him the best we can even if he doesn't notice it. And some of his officers, the new ones who weren't out in Montevideo with us, are mighty particular. Well, thank you, run along now. What are you waiting for? The money? The quarter-master will pay at the end of the week. Tell your father . . . What? Oh, your uncle, then—to let us have the week's account on Saturday. You needn't be afraid you won't get your money. The General is very particular that debts should be paid. And be here half an hour earlier tomorrow. *Avanti!* There's no room in these kitchens for any more boys. The ones we've got are trouble enough."

Italo swung up his empty basket and went out into the narrow street.

He stopped on the pavement just behind one of the Red-Shirt sentries, a splendid Tiger with long black curls falling to his shoulders. An officer in the uniform of the Bersaglieri came swaggering out of the door. A soldier in a Bersaglieri private's uniform brought his horse up for him, and held his stirrup while he mounted. A carriage drew up and a Triumvir in a black frock coat, with a broad red, green and white striped ribbon over one shoulder got out. He swept off his top hat as he crossed the threshold into the Villa. Next a Red-Shirt came out of the Villa and pulled a big watch out of his pocket to look at the time as he hurried away along the street.

It was all so interesting that Italo forgot about going home to the shop, even forgot that it was nearly time for lunch. He stooped down with his knees wide apart and his hands on his knees. He heard voices inside the doorway, several voices of men talking together. He saw the two sentries straighten their backs and square their shoulders. Italo peered eagerly past the long legs of the sentry in front of him, and saw three men in red shirts come out of the doorway. He recognized from thousands of pictures the one in the middle, the broad open forehead, the reddish hair and beard, the brilliant eyes, the sombrero, the bright handkerchief loosely knotted at the neck of the red shirt. Garibaldi! Garibaldi himself! Italo shook all over with excitement at seeing the great man so near.

A Red-Shirt came up with a gray horse for the General. Suddenly there was a whining noise overhead, and a crash. Italo found himself on the ground, smothered in a cloud of dust that blinded him, and filled his mouth and choked him so that he could not even cry out. For a moment everything seemed to be whirling round, and he did not know where he was. Then, as it steadied, he heard a voice say, "Take him inside. Call a doctor."

Italo thought this must be for him; he had a vague idea that he had been killed. The voice said again,

"There's a child there in the dust. See if he's all right."

Someone picked up Italo and set him carefully on his feet. He coughed and spat out the dust. Somebody wiped his face, and he could see again though his eyes twitched and smarted. He saw a lot of pieces of broken stone on the ground near him, with the dust still smoking from them. Garibaldi and the two men with him were wiping dust off their faces and shaking it off their clothes. The sentry was no longer standing in front of him, but two men were carrying him into the house. Italo cried out in dismay.

"He's not dead," somebody said. "Only stunned."

Italo sneezed and sneezed and then felt better.

"Not hurt?" Garibaldi said. "That's right. It was just another Pio Nono." Seeing Italo looked puzzled, he added, "That's what we call these little presents from the Pope's allies. What's your name, my lad?"

"Italo Strelli, *Signore*."

"Strelli? Are you any relation of Marco Strelli?"

"He's my brother, *Signore*."

"Marco Strelli is a fine soldier and a good patriot. Did you come here to see him?"

"No, *Signore*. I came to bring your salad. I work in my uncle's greengrocer shop."

"And now you've had a dusting from a Pio Nono, are you coming again tomorrow?"

"Yes. Every day," Italo said sturdily.

Garibaldi nodded. "That's right."

As he turned away Italo heard him say to one of his companions, "How can we be defeated when even the children show this spirit?"

Italo emptied the dust out of his basket, and hoisted it on to his shoulder. He was surprised to find that his legs felt rather shaky when he started off. They soon grew firm and steady again as he walked on, thinking with excitement of how Garibaldi had actually spoken to him and of what he had said about Marco, and of how he, Italo, would be able to tell them all about these things at home.

16

The Light in the Tower

"These Romans!" Marco exclaimed furiously. "They will not dig. We round up a party of citizens and take them outside the walls and put spades into their hands, so that they can dig earthworks for their own protection. But what do they do? If we take our eyes off them for five minutes they lie down and go to sleep, or they go home. These city people! Of what use would they be on a farm? If any trenches are dug at all it will be we, the Red-Shirts, who will have to dig them and we have plenty of other things to do."

Marco was pulling off his dusty boots as he spoke. He threw himself down on the bed.

"I have been digging or trying to make these clerks and shopkeepers dig all day, and tonight I have to go out on a sortie to try and find and destroy an outpost near the Vascello. The French are using it as a position for their sharpshooters to fire at the General when he is having his breakfast on the balcony of the Savorelli. *Mamma mia!* It is a miracle that they have not hit him already! Truly the Saints protect him!"

Italo said, "Uncle Bibi means to go and dig on Sunday when the shop is shut and I shall go with him."

"Uncle Bibi is too old and you are too young. It is the strong young men of the city who should be making earthworks such as the French have made. Then when the French advance we could place our guns in position behind the earthworks. But these lazy Romans won't do it. They say it is too hot."

Italo, who was standing in the window, said, "Here is that Benito Lupini coming to see us."

"I must sleep for an hour." Marco rolled over on to his back. "I did not stop for a siesta. Tell Benito to go away."

Not at all unwilling to tell Benito to go away, Italo ran down to the sitting-room over the shop, but he found that Uncle Bibi was there pouring out a glass of vermouth for Benito.

"Would you like a little glass too, Italo?" Uncle Bibi asked.

"No, thank you." Italo was not going to drink with Benito who had thought him a traitor.

"*Ciao*, Italo," Benito said. "What is the news from Pontevera?"

As Italo did not answer, Uncle Bibi replied, "Marco and Italo had a letter last week from Clara. All are well on the farm and Clara is affianced to Danielo Crevi."

"When the war is over," Benito said, "we will all go home to Pontevera and dance at the wedding."

Uncle Bibi said sadly, "I do not think that this war will be over for many years. Rome may fall, the French may restore the Pope to power in Rome, but such a thing as this *Risorgimento,* which so many young men believe in and are ready to die for, cannot be finished by one battle."

"You think that Rome will fall?" Benito asked uneasily.

"I am afraid so. They say that the French are bringing up big siege guns from the coast. What defenses have we but our crumbling old walls that could easily

99

be destroyed? In the end Mazzini and Garibaldi will have to surrender. I am told the Triumvirs wish it now, and only those two stop them."

"What you say is true," Benito said thoughtfully. "Perhaps it was a mistake to try and defend Rome."

"I am not a young man," Uncle Bibi said. "I have lost my son. I do not want others to lose theirs. I should be content for the united, free Italy to come slowly with the passing of years, as I think in the end it must come. But I know that young men like you and Marco cannot agree with me. You think your lives are of no value compared with the cause you are fighting for."

"Yes, yes, of course we think that," Benito said, smirking in a self-satisfied way.

"I don't believe *you* do," Italo muttered under his breath. Italo was quite sure that Benito had got himself made a storekeeper because he did not want to do any fighting, and that he cared more about himself than about a free and united Italy.

Benito shifted from one foot to another. The sharp stare of Italo's black eyes often made him feel uncomfortable. He asked, "Where is Marco?"

"He is sleeping," Italo said. "He has been digging all day without a siesta. He has to go out tonight to try and destroy one of the French outposts near the Vascello."

"Near the Vascello?"

"Yes, an outpost from which the French sharpshooters take aim at Garibaldi when he is on the balcony of the Savorelli."

Benito nodded. "Yes, the General takes terrible risks; he does not seem to be aware of them. Tell Marco to be careful. The French have many outposts on the hillside above the Vascello. I must go now, I have business waiting for me. Thank you for the drink, Signor Fantoni. *Ciao. Ciao,* Italo."

Benito went tramping down the stairs.

"Italo, you are not very polite to Benito who comes from your own district," Uncle Bibi said.

"No," Italo answered.

"We will have supper later tonight," Uncle Bibi said, "so that Marco can sleep. He will not be going out until after dark."

"I am going out after dark, too," Italo said importantly.

"Where are you going?"

"To the apartment of the English artists. They have asked me to come and see the lights of the French camp from their window."

"No doubt it is a show for them," Uncle Bibi said with some bitterness. "But they are good men," he added. "You are lucky to have these kind friends."

"I am kind to them, too," Italo said. "I pick out the freshest lettuces and the ripest cherries for them; that is, of course, after you have chosen the General's."

When they had finished supper Marco went off to the Gate of San Pancrazio to meet the scouting party who were going with him. Italo walked a little way with Marco, and then turned aside into the streets that he knew so well.

In the warm, dark summer night, he could hear the distant rattle of occasional musketry fire outside the walls and once the French bugles blowing from the Corsini. In a fortnight everybody in Rome had grown accustomed to these noises, and to the chance that a cannon ball might land at any time of day on one of the houses near the walls. It seemed as though it was almost a part of ordinary life to have a large French army encamped on the Janiculum, so near that the citizens of Rome could even hear shouted words of command when the wind was in the right direction.

In the artists' apartment Italo found Roger writing a letter and Bill making coffee. The room had its usual smell of coffee and paint and turpentine. Italo knew this smell by now and found it welcoming. There was a half-finished picture of a girl on the easel. The floor was covered with pieces of light stuff which Roger had dragged out of a drawer when he wanted to find something to drape round his model.

"Come along, Italo," Bill said. "Come and have some of the English plum cake that Roger's mother sent us from England, and then you shall have a good look at the lights."

Italo ate a slice of dark, rich, plummy spice cake, something he had never tasted before.

"Roger's mother read in the paper about the siege of Rome," Bill explained. "She thought it was the kind of siege where the city is surrounded on all sides, and food runs short. She did not understand that the French are only threatening Rome on one side. She was afraid we might be starving, so she sent this cake by a cousin who came here to work in the English Embassy. Roger is writing now to tell her that we have enough to eat, and that we have a special friend, a greengrocer called Italo, who brings us fresh fruit and vegetables every day. Now come and see the lights."

Italo moved across to the window and curled himself up on the seat under it. There was a whole line of lights all along the top of the earthwork which the French had dug in front of the Corsini.

Roger finished writing his letter and came, too, to look.

"They don't fire at the Savorelli at night," he said in his slow Italian.

"Garibaldi doesn't sleep there," Italo explained. "He goes there very early in the morning and stays there very late, but he sleeps in the barracks."

"I suppose the French know that," Bill said, "so it's only worth while aiming at the Savorelli in the daytime. They are knocking it to pieces by degrees, and the other houses near are not much better off. Except for one. Italo, do you know the name of the villa next to the Savorelli along the wall? It is quite big, too, and has a tower like the Savorelli. But we noticed when we were strolling round that way yesterday that this one villa had hardly been touched. We wondered what family it belonged to. It must belong to somebody near the Pope, I think, perhaps to one of the Cardinals, and the Pope must have asked the French not to destroy it. It is the only house they have spared near the Savorelli and it would be an easy mark. It has a tower nearly as high as that on the Savorelli. Do you know the name of the villa?"

"No."

"Next time you go to the Savorelli, take a look at it. It is on the south side of the Savorelli. The grilles over its windows are painted blue, and so are the shutters, but the paint is peeling off. It looks as though the villa had been neglected lately. Ask somebody what it is called."

"I will ask," Italo promised readily. He liked finding out things.

He was gazing entranced out of the window. His rooftop world looked so different in the dark. "There's a light in the tower," he said suddenly.

"What, of the Savorelli? There always is."

"No, of the villa next to it, the one you want to know about, the one the French don't shoot at."

Bill came to look out over Italo's shoulder. "So there is. I haven't seen a light there before."

"Somebody must live there."

"A caretaker, I expect. He must be a brave man to remain with cannon balls battering the houses on either side of him. But perhaps he knows that the villa he is looking after is under somebody's protection. Just out of curiosity I should like to know who it is who can stop the French from destroying his house."

"I'll try and find out."

"Tomorrow," Bill said, "Roger and I are going to dig earthworks outside the walls."

"But this is not your war," Italo said.

"I know, but we are almost coming to feel as if it were. And when our friends are in a tight corner we must do something to help."

Italo felt very pleased that his two dear friends from another country wanted to help the Red-Shirts.

"I'll tell you what you must do," he cried. "You must find two beautiful Italian girls here in Rome, rich girls whose fathers have palaces here, and you must each marry one and then you can live here always."

"Thank you, Italo," Bill said, laughing. "It's a very good idea. You find the two beautiful girls and we will marry them, and then if the French haven't knocked down the palaces everything will be splendid. We're going out to a café now so we'll walk part of the way home with you."

The house was dark when Italo got home. He crept up the two flights of stairs to his room, and was soon in bed and asleep.

When Italo woke, the early morning daylight was coming in at the window. He could see a piece of the sky flushed with sunrise. It was a footstep on the stairs that had wakened him so early. He sat up in bed as the door opened and Marco stumbled into the room. Without a word he lurched across to his bed and dropped on to it as if he was too tired to go any further.

"Marco," Italo called. "Are you all right? Are you hurt?"

"No, I'm not hurt."

"Did you get the outpost?"

"No. Four of the six men who went with me were killed. I and the two others have been dodging the French about the slopes all night. We had no chance. We were creeping up the path, and we were near to the outpost, when it seemed that the whole hillside of the Janiculum opened fire on us. You would have thought that they were expecting us. Now be quiet, Italo."

Still in his battle-stained red shirt and without getting beneath the sheets, Marco at once fell asleep. In a minute or two, as if they were under the roof of the farmhouse at home, Italo heard his deep breathing.

17

A Big Empty House

"Which villa are you talking about?" the cook asked. He added, "You haven't brought me many strawberries to-day."

"They were spoilt by the thunderstorm," Italo explained. "My uncle did not think they were good enough for the General so he did not buy many when the carts came in."

"No one can help a thunderstorm," the cook agreed kindly. "You are a good boy, you always come regularly and punctually. Now that boy who brings the fish, if they are firing on the Savorelli he will not come near. I have to send one of the kitchen boys out to look for him and take his basket from him on the other side of the street. What was it you were asking me about a villa?"

"The name of the big villa with a tower, the next one as you go along the road away from the Porta Pancrazio. It has a tower like this one, and blue-painted shutters."

"Oh, that. That is the Villa Manselli. It belongs to the Count Manselli, but I believe he has not lived there for a year or two now. He lives at his palace in Venice."

"But somebody looks after the villa for him?"

"There was a caretaker when we first moved into the Savorelli, but he and his wife moved out as soon as the French started firing. They were an old couple, and they were frightened of the French guns. They said they had had enough of Rome and were going back to their village to live with their daughter. No, that villa's empty. I daresay the General will take it over for headquarters; if the French knock many more holes in this one we shan't be able to use it much longer. Now listen, tomorrow I shall want plenty of small squash, and some eggplant. Tell your uncle."

Italo went out with his empty basket into the hot sunshine. There was an explosion and the noise of falling stone on the far side of the Savorelli, but he was now so well used to this that he hardly took any notice.

A narrow lane running back to the old walls of Rome divided the Villa Savorelli from the Villa Manselli. A high wall surrounded the Manselli. Italo walked round to the front and tried the big iron gates, from which the blue paint had mostly flaked off during the hot summers. He pressed his face against the iron bars and looked through.

There was a stone courtyard in front of the house where empty tubs stood. They had probably once held orange or lemon trees, but now there was only some dry crumbling earth in them. The big doors of the villa were shut, and the shutters were fastened over all the windows.

Italo walked on along the front of the villa and turned round the corner into another street that ran back to the walls of the city. Here half way down there was another, narrower gate in the high wall of the Villa Manselli. Italo looked through this and saw a side door in the house, also fastened. There was no sign of any life about the place. It seemed as though nobody had been in since the caretakers had fled.

Italo was disappointed. He had hoped to have something interesting to tell his friends, but the Villa Manselli was just an empty old house. Remembering that he was hungry and that it was nearly lunchtime, he ran off home.

He found Uncle Bibi just going to shut up the shop for the midday rest. He nodded to Italo.

"There you are. I was uneasy about you; with all this firing at the Savorelli I am always glad when you are back. Did the cook understand about the strawberries?"

"Yes, and he wants a lot of small squash and eggplant tomorrow."

Renato, the barber, came hurrying across the road.

"Wait a minute, Bibi," he called out. "Do not shut up for a minute. I have just heard some news. What do you think? The French have sent a small party with a flag of truce to Mazzini and the Triumvirs. They had sent to say that they have brought up their siege guns from the coast and they are not in position. They will give Mazzini twenty-four hours in which to surrender. If he does not do it before the end of the time, they will open fire on Rome. *Mamma mia!* What shall we do? Our houses will be destroyed, and we shall all be killed! Do you think that Mazzini will surrender? Do you?"

"Of course he won't!" Italo said proudly.

"It is all very well for the young to talk like that," Renato wailed. "It is another thing for us who have built up our businesses and have lived in Rome all our lives. Where can we go? What can we do?"

"We can do nothing," Uncle Bibi said, "until we see what happens. What will be will be." He looked at Italo. "But I am not sure that I shall not send Italo back to his father and mother in the country."

"No, no," Italo cried out. "How can you do that? The General must have his vegetables. My English friends must have their salads. I cannot go."

"And what will your mother say to me if I keep you

here while the French guns are firing on the whole city? I shall ask Marco when he comes in what he thinks."

Italo replied, "Marco knows that I, too, belong to Young Italy. He will not send me away when I am useful to Garibaldi."

"Which reminds me," Uncle Bibi said, "that you have not taken anything this morning for your English friends."

"No, because they will be out digging in front of the Pancrazio Gate. They asked me to bring their fruit this evening."

When Italo went round in the evening to the Via Barberina, Bill was lying exhausted on the settee with his long legs hanging over the end. Roger could be heard splashing in the bath in their bedroom next door.

"We dug!" Bill said. "How we dug! It was time I had some exercise. I ache in every joint after it. But in this heat! And there were so few of us there to do it. What is the matter with your Romans? Do they not take this war seriously?"

"They are sure of a surrender," Roger called through the door.

"The Pope and the French want one, of course. They do not want to destroy Rome. But they must know it will not be easy to make Mazzini agree to it. We had a message from the English Embassy today advising us to leave Rome."

"Are you going?" Italo asked in dismay.

"Not yet, anyhow. We want to see what happens."

Roger came in, rubbing himself dry with a bath towel.

"*Ciao*, Italo," he said. "I'm glad you have brought our salad. I could eat an ox roasted whole."

"I have a big steak all ready to grill when you are ready," Bill said.

Italo was turning to go away when he remembered something.

"The house you were asking about, *Signori,* the one with the tower next to the Villa Savorelli, is the Villa Manselli. The family have not lived there for a year or two, and the caretakers have fled. It it just a big empty house, with no one in it."

"That may be so," Bill said, "but I swear I saw a light in the tower again yesterday evening."

18

The Breach in the Wall

"Go to the Savorelli earlier today," Uncle Bibi said to Italo. "The Twenty-four Hour Truce that the French offered expires at noon. If Mazzini and the Triumvirs decide to surrender I suppose the French will march into the city. There will be great crowds and confusion. Some of the Red-Shirts may still try to resist. I would rather have you at home. If we don't surrender, the French may start to bombard the city with their siege guns at once. They are sure to aim at the Savorelli. I don't want you to hang about there. If you go now you will have plenty of time to get back here well before noon."

Italo hoisted the big basket full of strawberries and squash and eggplant on to his shoulder, and set off for the Savorelli.

As always when something important was happening, people were standing about outside the cafés, talking fast and waving their hands. They looked anxious and frightened.

"These city folk," Marco had said the night before. "All they want is to be comfortable. They shout '*Evviva*' to Garibaldi as he goes along the street, but they are not willing to take any risks for a free and united Italy."

It was quiet that morning at the Savorelli. There

were not many people going in and out of the big doors. The two sentries on duty stood carelessly, talking to one another. Italo took his vegetables round to the kitchen entrance.

The cook, who liked Italo, said, "If you stay a few minutes in front of the Villa you will see Garibaldi arrive home from the Assembly. He has gone there for the debate on the French demand for surrender."

"Do you think we shall surrender?" Italo asked.

"What? Our General surrender? No, he would never agree to that. Why, I was with him for four years in South America, in Montevideo, and we were in a hundred tight places, but he always found a way out without surrendering. Run round to the front now and you will see him again, and Mazzini, too. Mazzini is coming here to lunch with the General after the meeting of the Assembly. Of course," the cook added in a tone which he meant to be sarcastic, but which was really proud, "of course, the General must have a luncheon party on the day when the French may start firing on his headquarters with their siege guns. It is nothing to the General if cannon balls are dropping around him. He would never notice them."

Italo went round to the front of the villa and perched in the shade on a heap of fallen stones. He had entirely forgotten what Uncle Bibi had said to him about getting back to the shop in good time. Soon Italo heard cheering. A crowd of people appeared at the end of the street leading to the villa. Then they parted and Garibaldi on his gray horse rode through, his black servant, Aguilar, on another horse behind him, and some of his staff also on horseback.

Garibaldi waved to the crowd, and called out, "No surrender! We fight or die for the Freedom of Italy!"

"*Evviva! Evviva* Garibaldi!" the crowd shouted.

Garibaldi saw Italo perched on the stones and waved his hand to him. Italo glowed with pride.

"*Evviva* Garibaldi!" he shouted.

Behind Garibaldi and his officers came a carriage, with one man sitting alone in it. He was thin with a soft, dark beard, a high forehead, and brilliant eyes.

"*Evviva! Evviva* Mazzini!" the crowd shouted.

Italo looked eagerly at the man who had founded Young Italy and started the whole idea of a free and united Italy.

He saw Garibaldi dismount and give his hand to Mazzini as he got down from the carriage. The sentries, standing now at attention, saluted. Garibaldi and his staff and Mazzini went inside.

Italo picked up his basket. The crowd, hoping to see Garibaldi and Mazzini appear at one of the windows of the Savorelli, were blocking the street opposite. Italo thought it would be quicker to go by another one. He walked along the front of the Villa Manselli, looking for the next turning. He glanced down the lane on the far side of the Manselli and then stopped. What had yesterday been an unbroken wall now showed in one place a jagged opening with a heap of broken stone in front of it. The wall around the Manselli had been hit by a cannon ball aimed at the house beyond it. Italo, as he looked, saw at once that it would be easy to get inside the wall.

He ran down the lane and climbed without difficulty through the jagged opening. He did not really know why he wanted to, except that Bill and Roger had made him curious about the Villa Manselli. And after all, getting over the wall was not going to do him much good. The doors of the house would still be locked. Every shutter was fastened, and would be bolted on the inside.

Because the back of the villa was the only part of it

that he had not seen from the street, Italo walked round there. There was a narrow garden between the villa and the old stone wall of the city. Behind the house there was a loggia with an awning covered with a great climbing rose tree. Half its flowers had gone back to wild roses from neglect. It was choked with briars; the petals of fallen roses made a thick carpet on the floor of the loggia. There was a doorway at the back of the loggia, between two shuttered windows. The door would be locked, of course, like the others. Italo went and tried it. The handle turned under his hand and the door began to open. It was not locked! Italo stepped inside.

He found himself in a long room filled with painted wooden furniture. The red-tiled floor had grown dull for want of anybody to polish it. The room smelt of dust. Treading lightly in his sandals Italo tiptoed across it.

The only light came from the door on to the loggia which he had left open. When he opened a door into another room he could see hardly anything of it. If it had not been that one slat of a shutter was broken at the end, letting in a thin shaft of sunlight, he would have been completely in the dark.

Italo moved very cautiously, not for any particular reason but because being alone in a shut-up, empty house was a creepy feeling. He stole across the big room and opened another door.

The hall into which it opened was not quite dark. All the ground floor windows were shuttered but there was a little round window high up over the front door of the house. It had a small shutter, but nobody had bothered to fasten it. In the dim light Italo saw marble statues, big pictures in heavy gold frames, and a wide staircase leading up to a gallery that ran round three sides of the hall.

"I'll go up and find the tower," Italo said to himself. It would be wonderful to be able to look across at the French camp from that height. Besides, he might be able to see why there was sometimes a light in the tower.

He skimmed upstairs, crossed a landing and went on up another staircase not so wide and grand as the first one.

As soon as Italo turned the corner of this staircase the light coming into the hall through the high window no longer helped him. He was completely in the dark, and had to feel his way. It was a bit frightening but also exciting. He went on climbing in the dark, holding out one hand before his face.

After a minute or two he saw dim light ahead of him. The staircase made a turn and brought him out on to an upper landing. Here one of the shutters had been left open an inch or two. Somebody had tied it with string so it could not open any wider, but there was enough light to show the landing. A steep, narrow staircase with stone steps climbed up from the landing at the far end.

This must be the way to the tower. Italo went to the staircase and began to climb. It was a winding staircase, and as soon as he turned the first corner he was again in the dark. It was more frightening this time because the walls were so close together that his elbows brushed against them on either side. This made him feel shut in. He climbed very slowly, a step at a time, feeling before him with one hand. Then, as he climbed, light began again and got brighter. Soon there were broad panels of sunlight on the stone wall ahead of him.

Italo skipped up the last flight of steps, and came out into a square room with windows back and front. There were no shutters over these windows, but somebody had hung a blanket over the one that looked towards Rome. The blanket did not quite cover it. If anybody had a light on in that room at night a chink would show down the side. This must be what Bill had noticed!

Italo went to the opposite window and looked out over the wall of Rome to the slopes of the Janiculum and the French earthworks hiding the Corsini gardens. On the roof-top of the Corsini, above the earthworks, he could see the French flag flying. Lower down, at the bottom of the hillside, the flag of Italy was flying on the Vascello, the Italian outpost. Italo had never seen the French camp from such a good vantage point. He could see the muzzles of guns sticking out of the earthworks, and a cluster of tents just showing. He pushed the window open and leaned out. Beyond where the earthworks stopped, he saw a small party of French cavalry in their blue uniforms and their *képis*, returning from a scouting foray.

He leaned out, enjoying the feeling of the hot sun on his head and neck after the darkness of the staircase and the dim light of the rooms. While he watched the French cavalry, all the clocks of Rome began to strike. The bells of the many churches rang for the Angelus, the prayer that was always said at noon.

Italo had forgotten all about the time. Uncle Bibi had told him to be back before noon. He must not stay here any longer. He look one more look at the French camp before he turned to go. Suddenly, there were puffs of white smoke from all the muzzles of the guns sticking out of the earthworks, and a noise like thunder rumbled all round. The truce was over. There had been no surrender. The French guns had begun to bombard Rome.

Italo felt rather frightened at being alone in a strange, empty house while this was happening. He wanted now to get home. He drew in his head and was making for the staircase when he stopped. He saw on the floor by the wall a row of lanterns. Beside them was a

116

basket-covered wine flask, and a packet of tallow candles. There was a pad of paper lying there, with some figures and other marks scribbled on the top sheet.

Italo, always curious, picked up one of the lanterns. The sides between the square iron frame were filled with red-tinted glass. He examined the next one, and found that the glass was green. A third had clear glass, and the fourth yellow.

For a minute Italo was puzzled, then he understood. This was why there had been a light in the tower after dark. Somebody had been signalling from the window. The signal could be seen easily from the French lines. There was a French spy in Rome.

19

A Man in the Half-light

He carefully put the lanterns back in a row against the wall exactly as he had found them. He thought for a minute of taking the writing pad with him to show to somebody. Then he decided against it. It would be better for the spy not to know that anybody had been in the tower. Then he would go on signalling and there would be a chance to catch him at his work. To run as fast as possible and tell Marco was the thing now.

Italo sprang down the narrow tower staircase. After the bright sunlight above he could hardly see anything on the landing below, which was lit only by the narrow shaft of daylight that came through the window where the shutter was tied back. Italo stood still for a minute, blinking his eyes. Then he heard a sound in the house below him, and another. Somebody was there! Somebody was coming up the lowest flight of stairs.

Italo looked wildly round for a hiding place. All the doors along this landing were shut and would probably be locked. There was no time to find out; he might make a noise if he tried to open one. There was a chest against the wall at the other end of the landing where the light barely reached. Italo ran noiselessly towards it, and crouched down on the far side of it, flattening his thin body into the corner between the chest and the wall. It was not a safe hiding place but it was the best that he could find.

Italo heard the footsteps coming up the second flight of stairs. He prayed to the Mother of God and all the Saints to make this man who must be the spy go straight up to the tower without looking along the corridor.

The footsteps came nearer and nearer to the top of the stairs. Italo could hear his own heart beating. He squeezed himself more tightly into his corner, and peered cautiously round the end of the chest. He saw a man step on to the dim landing, cross it swiftly and vanish in the opening of the tower staircase.

Italo gasped with shock. The half light of the landing had been enough to show him that the man was wearing a red shirt. He had also had a swift impression that the figure seen for two or three seconds at the other end of the long, dimly lighted corridor was the figure of Benito Lupini.

Italo waited until he heard the footsteps reach the top of the tower staircase. Then he came out of his hiding place and stole swiftly along the landing. He saw now that there was another staircase half-way down, which probably led to the kitchens. He did not wait to explore any further. He pulled off his sandals and swung them round his neck. Then silently, on his bare feet, he crept down the two lower flights of stairs, across the empty rooms and out on to the loggia. He ran round the house, crawled over the broken place in the wall and into the street again.

He drew a deep breath of relief when he was out of the house. At once everything in it began to seem rather unreal, as if he had waked up in the morning after a strange dream.

He remembered again that Uncle Bibi had told him to be home by noon. He put on his sandals and ran quickly through the streets. The thunder of the French guns was still shaking the sky. The streets were empty. People had gone inside their houses, as if they felt that the thinnest wall would be some protection against a bombardment that might come their way at any minute. Far off along the city wall there was the crash of falling stone. Italo hardly noticed it. He was trying to make up his mind what he was going to do.

When he came near to the shop he saw Uncle Bibi standing in the doorway watching for him. As soon as he saw Italo, Uncle Bibi waved to him to hurry.

"What have you been doing, Italo? It is half-past twelve, and I told you to be back here by noon. I have been worried about you since the bombardment started. You have been away nearly two hours."

"I am sorry," Italo said. "I waited to see Garibaldi and Mazzini come back to the Savorelli from the Assembly. Garibaldi saw me and waved to me. There was a crowd with him blocking the streets. I had to go round another way to get home."

As soon as he had said this he wondered why he hadn't at once told Uncle Bibi about the signalling lanterns and Benito Lupini in the empty villa. But something stopped him from speaking; Benito Lupini was part of his private vendetta.

Uncle Bibi hurried Italo upstairs.

"Come and eat, come and eat. Your aunt has been down to tell me that her dish was spoiling and that we should not wait for you, but I could not begin until I knew that you were back safe."

Italo sat down at the table and plunged his fork into his plateful of spaghetti. He was very hungry, but he did not feel inclined to chatter as he usually did. He ate without speaking.

"Marco came in for a minute," Uncle Bibi said. "So far the French seem to be firing only on two bastions of the walls. They are the two weakest; they must somehow have known about them. We shall not be seeing Marco for a day or two. He has gone to take charge of a party rebuilding the Eighteenth Bastion. They will have to work day and night. Marco said that the sentries of the National Guard go home for a rest whenever they feel like it, and the Red-Shirts dare not take their eyes off them. Well, let us eat; today we have food. But the French are said to have dammed the stream on the Janiculum that turns the wheels of the flour mills, so whether we shall have bread in a few days' time no one knows."

After lunch Italo went upstairs as usual and lay down on his bed for the siesta. The day was very hot and he was tired after the excitement of the morning, but he could not go to sleep. The French guns were making so much noise pounding the bastions, but it was not only that. Italo had to make up his mind what he was going to do about the spy in the Villa Manselli.

If Marco had been here he would have told him all about it. He knew what Marco would say he ought to do. He ought to go at once and tell the Red Shirts at the Villa Savorelli. They would go into the Manselli and take possession of the tower. There would be no more signalling. But they might not catch the spy. If it was Benito Lupini he was cunning. He might slip through their fingers. Italo could not bear this to happen. He had for so long been angry with Benito on his own account that he felt that the most important thing was to catch him out.

Italo thought, rolling about on his bed until he was sticky with heat and the blanket had wrinkled into hard creases underneath him. If only he could make quite certain that it was Benito. If only he could tell the Red-Shirts when Benito was there, actually in the tower, so that they could go in and catch him with the signalling lanterns in his hand.

Gradually a plan took shape in Italo's mind. The spy would not use the lanterns for signalling till after dark. After dark would be the time to bring the Red-Shirts to the tower. Italo decided that he himself would slip out of this house when it was nearly dark and find some place near the back entrance of the Manselli. He would watch for the spy to come and make certain that it was Benito. Then he would run across to the Savorelli and give the alarm. He hugged himself joyfully, imagining Benito crouching in the Tower Room with his lanterns, and a posse of Red-Shirt soldiers running up the last narrow flight of stairs to catch him in a trap.

Italo grew tired of trying to go to sleep. He rolled off his tumbled bed, and went down to the room over the shop. It was shuttered to keep out the mid-day heat, but one shutter was a little open. Zelinda had opened it. She was sitting on the window-seat sewing some of the fine white embroidery that the nuns were teaching her. The nuns had closed the school when the bombardment started, and were putting their mattresses up at the windows again.

Zelinda was tired of sitting and sewing alone; she was pleased to see Italo. He came and sat down beside her. He wished he could have told her about his morning's adventure, but she was a chatterbox. She told everything to her mother. It wouldn't do to let anyone know yet. Still, there would be no harm in letting Zelinda know that something interesting was going on.

Italo said, "It's a pity that you're too young to keep a secret."

"I'm not too young! I know a lot of secrets. The girls at school tell them to me."

"Oh, girls' secrets." Italo was scornful. "Those aren't important."

"Yes, they are. Just as important as boys' secrets. What's so important about this one of yours?"

"I'm not thinking about a boy's secret," Italo said mysteriously. "This is a man's secret."

"Then why did anybody tell it to you? You're a boy, not a man."

"Nobody told it to me. I found out for myself."

"You're very inquisitive," Zelinda said primly. "Mamma says so."

"Of course I want to know things. And if everybody knew what I know now—" Italo stopped and shook his head solemnly. "If you were a bit older, Zelinda, if you were twelve like me, perhaps, I might trust you, but you're only eleven."

Zelinda said huffily, "I'm not interested in your secret. I don't want to know. I expect it's something very silly."

"I can tell you this," Italo said. "It's a secret that even Garibaldi would want to know."

"Why don't you go and tell him, then, and leave me alone?"

This question made Italo feel uncomfortable. He knew really that to tell Garibaldi or some of his Red-Shirts at once about the spy in the tower was what he ought to do. To forget his uncomfortable feelings he became even more boastful.

"What would you say, Zelinda, if I tell you that I have my enemy in my power?"

"I should say that you were making up a story. Who is your enemy? You ought not to have enemies, except of course the French. Father Justino would tell you to forgive your enemy. He would give you a penance until you did. He did that to me when I quarrelled with Marta for three weeks without stopping."

"You're a girl." Italo could not resist letting her get near his secret. He said impressively, "My enemy is somebody you know."

Zelinda considered. "Is it one of the boys in the square?"

"It's not a boy at all. It's a man."

"Does Marco know him?" Zelinda admired Marco so much that anything he knew about at once became more interesting.

"Yes, Marco knows him. But Marco doesn't know this secret about him."

"It can't be a very important secret if Marco doesn't know it."

This was so annoying that Italo might have been tempted to tell her more, but at that moment Uncle Bibi came into the room.

"Time to open the shop again, Italo," he said. "Will you unlock the door? There's a woman waiting outside now. See what she wants, and I'll come down in a minute."

The clocks of Rome chimed three and the French guns boomed out again as Italo ran downstairs.

20

Capture

The French guns stopped firing at sunset. It was suddenly very quiet in Rome; you could hear voices and footsteps again.

"The noise has given me a headache," Uncle Bibi said. "We will all go to bed early."

This suited Italo. After he was supposed to be in bed he stole downstairs and very quietly let himself out of the side door.

"They will never know. I shall be back long before morning," he said to himself as he slipped out into the street.

It was not yet completely dark, but it would be by the time Italo got to the Villa Manselli. He knew that he must hurry if he was to make sure of catching the spy. The June night was cooler than the day, but it was still very hot. People were coming out of their houses now the bombardment had stopped; the café tables on the pavement were beginning to fill up. On the whole the Romans were relieved to find that so far only the walls had been the target for the French. They began to talk and laugh in the cafés much as usual. Italo, quick and light on his feet, dodged the groups who were clustering on the pavements, and sped past the full tables.

"Italo! Where are you off to in such a hurry?" It was

Bill who, as he spoke, caught Italo by the elbow. Roger, with a cigar in his mouth and his sketchbook under his arm, was standing beside him.

"We're just going to our usual café. Come and have a cup of coffee with us," Bill said.

For the first time Italo was not glad to see his English friends.

"I must go. I've got to take a message," he panted.

He jerked his elbow free of Bill's hand, and raced off along the street. As he turned the corner he saw Bill and Roger strolling on towards their café.

It was quite dark when he reached the Savorelli. There were lights in all the windows of Garibaldi's headquarters. Red-Shirts, officers of the Bersaglieri and men in frock coats were still going in and out of the big doors.

One of the sentries on duty was a Red-Shirt whom Italo had made friends with, and who always grinned at him when he went round with his basket to the kitchen. Italo stopped for a minute. He wondered if he should tell this sentry about the spy in the tower. But he still wanted first to make sure it was Benito and to bring the Red-Shirts to catch him busy with his lanterns. He walked away from the brightly lit Savorelli and passed the dark front of the Manselli. He turned down the narrow side street towards the gap in the wall.

Here it was very dark; there were no lamps in the side street. The noise and bustle outside the Savorelli suddenly seemed far away. Italo was alone, going to look for his enemy. He suddenly began to feel frightened. He had said grandly to Zelinda that his enemy was in his power, but he saw now that unless he was very careful it could turn out to be the other way round. He felt little shivers run over his body in spite of the warm night.

He stole along close to the wall, running his hand lightly over the stone so as to feel the gap that he would not be able to see. The stone was still warm from the day's sun. Italo's fingers found space. He climbed cautiously over the broken stones, testing each foothold before he rested his foot on it. Once a stone slipped under his feet and he stopped, holding his breath, until the noise it made had died away. At last he was standing on the ground inside the wall.

He crept along the side of the house until he reached the corner and sidled round it. Here he remembered there were some wooden steps leading up to the loggia. One of them creaked even under his light weight. He waited at the top of the steps, listening. He heard only the distant noises of the city, voices and footsteps, the clop-clop of horses' hooves and the sound of a church bell ringing.

He tiptoed across the loggia and put his hand on the fastening of the door. It was still not locked. Either the spy was very careless or the key had been lost long ago. Italo opened the door and slipped inside.

The darkness inside the house was different from the darkness out of doors. It was thick, heavy, frightening.

Italo's plan had seemed very easy to carry out when he was lying on his bed at home. Now it began to seem difficult. The spy might have come already. He might now be busy with his lanterns in the tower room. Or he might not come tonight at all. How long would Italo have to wait alone in the dark house to see if he was coming? How long could he bear to wait? Already the sweat was running down his body under his shirt. He felt that at any moment the panic growing inside him would swell into a great ball, and burst, so that he would run headlong out of the house. If only there was somebody with him! If only he were back in his room at Uncle Bibi's or safe in the farm at home!

Remembering the farm at home made him remember Benito, who had told lies about him so that he had to leave it. He grew angry again, and his fear shrank to a size that he could manage. He crept forward feeling his way into the next room.

There was a lot of furniture there. He came up against a table, and when he moved away from it his hands feeling before his face found some silky stuff hanging down which must be one of the window curtains. Perhaps it would be easiest to feel his way round the wall from window to window until he came to the bottom of the stairs. He began to try this, and then stopped dead, almost stopped breathing. There were footsteps on the loggia outside.

Then he heard the door gently opened, and voices whispering. Italo was startled. It had never occurred to him that there could be more than one spy.

Now he knew how silly he had been to come here alone, silly and wrong. All he wanted now was to hide until the two spies had gone up to the tower, and then fetch the Red-Shirts.

The men stopped just inside the doorway. A voice that Italo recognized, said, "Give me a light."

Italo dodged behind one of the window curtains. He heard the scrape of a match. The silk of the curtain had rotted with age and damp and there were several slits in it. Italo put his eye to one and saw the yellow light from a lantern making a bright circle round two men.

He hugged himself with silent glee as he saw clearly the thin face and the long nose. It was Benito!

Benito took the lantern from the other man, who also wore a red shirt, and held it up above the level of his shoulder. He looked all round the room.

"Why was the door ajar?" he said to his companion. "I left it shut this morning."

The other man answered, "The catch didn't hold. They had let everything rot here."

Benito said, "All the same, Gino, I don't feel easy. Let's have a look round before we go up."

Italo grasped the folds of the silk curtain that hid him, and squeezed them tightly in his nervous excitement.

"I've had an uneasy feeling all day," Benito said. "I told you I found the door on to the loggia unlatched this afternoon."

Gino, a big, brawny fellow, replied in a bored voice, "You thought you'd fastened it last night and you hadn't. One can't see in the dark. It's this gunfire. It gets on one's nerves. After all, we can't be sure that the French won't hit their friends by mistake as well as their enemies. I've a good mind to come and camp out here. They'll be careful not to touch this house. It's far too useful to them."

"You'll do nothing of the sort," Benito said sharply. "You are much too careless. You'd show a light at a window or hang your head out of one or something."

Gino shrugged his shoulders. "Better come up to the tower. It must be getting near time."

They began to walk across the room.

Italo felt already a great wave of relief. In another minute or two they would have gone up the stairs, and he would slip out of the house and run, run round to the Savorelli and bring the Red-Shirts. And Benito would be caught, as he had hoped, signalling.

Benito and Gino were at the other side of the room now. In his frantic excitement Italo tugged harder at the curtain that he was still gripping. There was a loud sound of tearing silk. Half the curtain collapsed on top of Italo. He heard one of the men shout as he struggled frantically to free himself from the folds.

There were heavy footsteps and hard breathing near him. Arms seized him roughly, and pulled him away from the window. Light shone in his face, dazzling him. Strong hands gripped him.

He screamed and struggled, he fought like a frightened cat, but Gino was too strong for him, and gave him a cuff on the side of the head that for a moment half stunned him. Benito was holding the lantern so that the light shone full on him.

"Italo!" he said. "It's you! At your spying tricks again!"

"I'm not a spy," Italo cried furiously. "You are!"

"Who sent you?" Benito asked with a nervous quaver in his voice. "Is anyone waiting outside? Who knows that you are here?"

"No one sent me. I found you out myself."

As soon as he had said this Italo knew that he had made a mistake. They would know there was no one at hand to help him.

Gino muttered, "Better finish him off."

Benito said nervously, "He comes from my village. His brothers would avenge him." He added more firmly, "No, Gino. He's only a tiresome inquisitive boy. I've known him to do this sort of thing before. Better bring him up. We'll put him where he can do no harm."

Gino pulled the folds of the curtain, in which Italo was still struggling, over his head and face, and wound them round his body.

Half suffocated, Italo tried to struggle again, but, bundled up as he was, he was helpless. He could not even move his hand to get the silk off his face. He felt himself lifted in Gino's arms and carried upstairs. A door was opened and he was thrown down on a floor. Bumped and shaken, short of breath, he had no time to struggle clear of the curtain before he heard the key turn in the lock of the door. He was alone, lying on a tiled floor in the dark.

2 1

The Search

"But where can Italo have gone? Where can he have gone?" Aunt Maria wailed for the tenth time.

"Perhaps," Renato the barber suggested, "he was frightened by the bombardment yesterday, as anyone might be, and has run back to his home in the country."

"But without a word to us?" Uncle Bibi exclaimed. "And Italo is a brave boy! I have always been afraid that he would not be careful enough to keep under cover when he went to the Savorelli. Why should he run home without telling me? I should not have stopped him if he wished to go."

"Ah, but the young do not like to say when they are afraid." Renato shook his head. "Now, my Gian Franco, yesterday, he was helping to bring up stones to rebuild the Eighteenth Bastion, and when he came home at night he was as I have never seen him before, quite white and silent, because he had been in such danger all day for the first time in his life. He could eat only two little spoonfuls of *pasta*. I knew what it was, but he would only say that it was the heat and that the dust from the broken stones had got in his throat. No, the young they do not like to say they are frightened. So it may be that your Italo has slipped off to Pontevera without a word."

"It is not like him," Uncle Bibi said. "It is not like him."

"It is lucky for you," Renato said, "that today is the festival of St Peter so you will not have to open the shop without help; and by tomorrow, who knows?"

They were all talking in the doorway of the house. A woman came across the square towards them, dragging a boy of about seven by the hand.

"Good morning," she said. "I have heard that your Italo has not been at home all night and that you do not know where he has gone. My Basilio here saw him last night just before it was dark. He went out of the square into the Via San Ginese. Is that not right, Basilio? Tell the poor Signora Fantoni which way her nephew went."

Basilio, struck with sudden shyness, pointed towards the far corner of the square.

Basilio's mother gave him a shake. "Go on. Where is your tongue? Tell to the Signora Fantoni what you told me."

As Basilio only hung his head down and tugged to try and get his hand away from hers, his mother spoke for him.

"My Basilio said that Italo was running fast as if in a great hurry."

"Thank you, *Signora*," Aunt Maria said. "And you, too, Basilio; thank you for coming to tell us."

Basilio's mother led him off, scolding him as she went.

"By that way," Uncle Bibi said, "Italo might have been going to the Savorelli. But why should he go there again late last night? He had taken everything that was ordered in the morning."

"He loitered yesterday morning to see Garibaldi," Aunt Maria reminded them. "Do you not remember how late he was for lunch? Perhaps he ran back to see Garibaldi again at night."

133

"No, no," Renato persisted. "I think that he has run back home to the farm and was ashamed to say that he was going. It may be, you know, when he went to bed at night and thought that the guns would be firing again all next day, he wished for his mother and decided to return to her."

"No, no, that is not like Italo," Uncle Bibi repeated.

Zelinda came round the corner wearing her black school apron and a black lace veil that she had borrowed from her mother over her hair. She had been to Mass at the Convent with all the other pupils, but now the school was closed for the festival holiday. She joined the group in the doorway.

"Zelinda, dear," Renato said. "Can you not help us? Children talk to one another. Do you not know where Italo has gone?"

Zelinda looked astonished.

"He has not slept in his bed at all. We cannot find him anywhere," Aunt Maria explained.

"When I came into the room yesterday after the siesta," Uncle Bibi said, "Italo was talking to you. Did he say that he wanted to go home to the farm? Did he want to go away from the French guns?"

"Oh, no," Zelinda said at once. "He did not say anything about the guns or about going home." She added, "He said he had a secret."

"What kind of secret? Did he tell you what it was?"

"No." Zelinda made an impatient little movement of her veiled head. "He said it was a man's secret. He said Garibaldi would be glad to know it. He was talking nonsense. He said his enemy was in his power."

Uncle Bibi threw up his hands. "What secret or what enemy could he have? He must have been playing a game with you."

Zelinda, who thought she knew when a boy was talking grandly to impress her, nodded.

"I must go back to my shop," Renato said. "People do not buy vegetables on the festival day, but they must be shaved just the same. Have you heard that the Trium-virs have ordered a tremendous display of fireworks this evening just as usual? They are mad. Everyone is mad nowadays. Who knows that the French may not be in the city to snatch the fireworks out of our hands! My last customer told me that they pick out all the weak places in the walls to fire on as if they had them marked on a map. It is thought that there are spies among us. Let me know, Bibi, if Italo returns. When we go to Mass I will light a candle for his safety."

Renato went back across the street to his shop.

The French guns boomed out again.

"I must find Marco," Uncle Bibi decided. "I must tell him that Italo has disappeared. Ah, poor Rosa, poor Matteo, who trusted their son to me!"

Uncle Bibi walked through the streets towards the Eighteenth Bastion. It was strange to see people about in holiday clothes. Some houses and shops were hanging out their usual decorations for the festival of St Peter even though the French were so near on the opposite hill and their guns were at work battering the city walls again.

The Eighteenth Bastion was a scene of confusion. Many of the big stones that had been knocked off the wall had been reduced to rubble, but engineers were at work with a small crane trying to lift the bigger pieces back on to the walls again. Red-Shirts, men of the Roman guard and some of the workmen of the city were bringing up barrowloads of small stones and earth to stuff into the openings.

"Have you see Marco Strelli?" Uncle Bibi asked one of the Red-Shirts, who stopped to straighten his back and to take a swig from a wine flask that was standing in the shade of a big boulder.

"Marco Strelli? He is up there on top of the wall."

Uncle Bibi looked up and saw Marco in his red shirt outlined against the blue sky. Marco was directing the men who were placing the stones. Uncle Bibi began laboriously to climb up towards him.

"Marco! Marco!"

Marco looked down and saw his uncle. He sprang down in two great leaps.

"What is it?" he said. "I cannot leave this work. The French are firing on one of the other bastions at the moment and we have to a chance to rebuild here."

"Italo has gone. He slipped out of the house last night about eight o'clock and we have not seen him since."

"The young rascal! Give him a good beating when he comes back."

"But he may not come back. I am afraid that something has happened to him. Or do you think that he may have been frightened by the bombardment and have gone home to the farm?"

"No, no, he would not do that. He is off on some game of his own, but he will turn up again. Do not worry, Uncle. Italo can take care of himself. I cannot stay down here any longer." Marco took two leaps on to the top of the wall again. "Beat him well when he comes," he called over his shoulder.

There was nothing for Uncle Bibi to do but to go home, hoping to find that Italo had come back while he was away. But Aunt Maria, who was taking advantage of the holiday to clean out the shop, shook her head sadly.

"No, he has not come back. He must have gone home to Pontevera."

Renato came across the street.

"Do you know, Bibi, that tonight there are to be illuminations for the festival as well as the fireworks?

The whole of the square in front of St Peter's is to be lit with Bengal lights, red, emerald, and green. It has just been announced by order of the Assembly."

"*Diamine!* The Assembly are mad," Uncle Bibi exclaimed. "Is this a moment to waste time and money on illuminations when the French may bombard the whole city at any moment?"

"No, no, you are right, it is a foolish thing to do," Renato agreed hastily. He added, "You will not go to see the illuminations, I know, with all your troubles one would not expect it, and indeed I myself would never go on my own account, but my Gian Franco . . ."

"I thought your Gian Franco was helping to rebuild the walls," Aunt Maria struck in.

"He worked on the walls all day yesterday, but today he is so stiff and tired that he can hardly move. Tomorrow he will perhaps go and work again. But tonight he has begged his mother and me to take him to supper in a café, and to see the illuminations as we have always done on St Peter's Day. So, we shall go."

Uncle Bibi said kindly, "Of course a boy like Gian Franco wants to see the illuminations. If my Italo was only safe here I am sure that he would want to go, too. How shall I ever tell Rosa and Matteo if something dreadful has happened to him?"

As he spoke the French guns, which had been silent for half an hour, boomed out again. This time the sound was nearer.

"There," Uncle Bibi exclaimed, "they are firing again on the Eighteenth Bastion. One can tell by the direction from which the noise comes. And my other nephew, Marco, who is working on the bastion and never thinks of danger! You have indeed something to thank the Saints for, Renato, that your Gian Franco was too tired to go and work today!"

"We live in dreadful times here in Rome," Renato agreed. He went back across the road to his house.

"I shall go to the Villa Savorelli," Uncle Bibi said to Aunt Maria. "I shall ask if Italo went there last night. He has always said that the cooks were friendly and kind to him. One of them may have seen him. There can be no harm if I go round to the kitchen and ask."

It was very hot. Uncle Bibi, who always seemed to roll rather than to walk, had to stop several times to mop his face on the way through the streets. Once, as he paused, an old woman standing in her doorway smiled at him, and he spoke to her.

"Excuse me, *Signora,* but I wonder if you have ever seen a boy who must have passed your house every day lately carrying a basket of vegetables? A thin boy with very bright black eyes? It is my nephew who has not come home since he went out last night."

"No, *Signore,* I do not remember seeing any boy with a vegetable basket. There are so many boys, and since in this part of the city we are poor there are so many who are very thin, and many have black eyes."

"That is true," Uncle Bibi said sadly.

"But I will pray for you that he may return," the old woman said.

"Thank you, *Signora.*"

Uncle Bibi walked on towards the Savorelli.

He stopped in horror and surprise when he first came in sight of Garibaldi's headquarters. What had been a noble villa was now half in ruins. The tower had been destroyed, the two upper stories of the house were a crumbling ruin, there was no glass left in any of the windows. Garibaldi's flag was no longer flying from the roof.

As Uncle Bibi stood staring, two men in red shirts came out of the front doorway each carrying a load of bedding and cooking pots on their backs. They heaped these on the dusty pavement where two more Red-Shirts loaded them into a cart.

Uncle Bibi approached the man in charge of the cart, who was giving the horse something to eat out of a nose-bag.

"Excuse me, *Signore,* but is this no longer the General's headquarters?"

"As you see we are leaving it. The French have not left enough standing. They fired on the house for an hour early this morning."

"You have not seen a boy? A boy of twelve, who used to come here with vegetables for the General's table? It is my nephew, and he has disappeared. He went off last night and he has not come back this morning."

"A boy? We had too much to do to notice boys," the Red-Shirt answered roughly. Then, seeing Uncle Bibi's distress, he added, "I expect he has gone somewhere to work with those who are repairing the walls. There are some civilians helping, but they soon get tired of it when they find it isn't a picnic. Your nephew will be back before long if he is one of those."

"The cook here would know him," Uncle Bibi said desperately. "Perhaps I could ask the cook?"

"The cooks have gone on to prepare food for the General and his staff at the barracks."

"I am so much afraid that our Italo may have been hit by a chance shot."

"Chance shot?" the Red-Shirt said bitterly. "There are no chance shots! These accursed French know exactly what they are aiming at. Look at this house." He waved his hand at the battered Savorelli. "And look at the next one." He pointed to the Manselli, still standing almost untouched behind its high walls. "Oh, no, the French are clever. They are not shooting to destroy

Rome. They are shooting to frighten those fools, the Triumvirs, peacocking about in their top hats and their red, white and green sashes. The French are shooting for a surrender, that's what they are shooting for. But you can take my word for it, Garibaldi will never surrender. He would sooner march out with all of us, all his army, and let the French have Rome." The Red-Shirt added, "I am sorry about your nephew, but there's so much for a boy to see at the moment in this city. I expect he's somewhere about gaping. He'll come home when he's hungry, you'll see. You'll probably find him there when you get back."

Uncle Bibi clung to this hope all through the hot walk home, but as soon as he entered the house he saw by the faces of Aunt Maria and Zelinda that there was no news.

"No," they said in answer to his inquiring eyes. "Alas, no, Italo has not come home."

22

Rescue Party

"There, that's finished," Roger said.

It was the picture of the old woman sitting in the doorway, which Italo had thought dull. Bill came to look at the canvas.

"It's the best you've done," he said warmly. Roger stretched his arms above his head, and yawned.

"I think so, too. I feel like sleeping for a week after it."

"You don't want to go to the square to see the illuminations?"

"I don't feel much like illuminations. It's clear the game is up for Garibaldi. The French will break in through one of the gaps in the walls, and the Assembly will have to surrender."

"What will happen to Garibaldi?"

"I should think he will have to go into exile again. There will be a free and united Italy one day, but this attempt has failed."

Roger began to clean his brushes. Bill put his own drawing back in his portfolio.

"Shall we go out for supper, or eat here?"

"Have we any food?"

"We've got some cold meat, and cheese and wine, but no fruit or vegetables."

"What has happened to our friend Italo, I wonder?"

"I suppose his uncle has kept him busy with other things."

"It's not like Italo to forget us. He may still come."

"No, of course he won't," Bill exclaimed. "Now I come to think of it, the shop will be shut today for the holiday. I expect Italo will be going to see the illuminations."

"Let's eat what we have, and then go out for some coffee."

"Very well."

Bill got up and began to rummage in the cupboard where they kept their food. Roger strolled to the window and looked out over the roof tops.

"It's getting dark early tonight," he said. "There's no air anywhere. I think there's going to be a storm."

"To douse the illuminations."

"There's a light in the tower of that house again," Roger said. "The house next to the Villa Savorelli."

"I heard in the café that Garibaldi has had to evacuate the Savorelli. The French knocked it to bits early this morning."

Roger came back to the table and cut himself a plate of meat.

"I shall be glad when the whole thing is over now. It's a sad business watching the defeat of brave men fighting in a good cause."

They were just finishing their supper when they heard footsteps on the stairs.

"Hullo!" Bill said. "We're going to have visitors."

There was a knock at the door. When Bill opened it he saw Uncle Bibi in the doorway with a tall, dark young man in a red shirt behind him.

"Excuse me, please, *Signori*," Uncle Bibi said. "I hope you will forgive me for interrupting you. We have come, my nephew Marco and I, to ask if you have seen Italo?"

"Not since last night when we ran into him for a minute in the Via San Ginese. Why?"

"*Signori*, he has disappeared. He slipped out last night after we had all gone to bed, and we have not seen him since."

Bill began to translate for Roger, but Roger said, "It is all right, I understand." He was beginning to be able to follow when people spoke in Italian, though he was slow in speaking it.

Bill said, "Italo would not stop to talk to us. He said that he was taking a message."

Uncle Bibi threw up his hands. "A message? But what message? And to whom?" He added, "Marco is the brother of Italo. He has just come off duty on the wall for a few hours. It was he who suggested that we should ask you, since you have always been very kind to Italo. The boy might perhaps have spoken to you of some plan that he had in his head."

"No, I don't think he did," Bill said slowly. "Last time he came here it was in the evening to see the lights of the French camp from our window. He always likes looking at the roofs of the city from here."

"He has never spoken to you, *Signori*, of a secret? He talked to my little girl of one a few hours before he went off."

"No, we never heard anything about his secrets," Bill said. "I am very sorry that you are worried about him. I expect he will turn up. I wish we could help you to find him. We are fond of Italo."

"He is a good boy," Uncle Bibi agreed. "It is not like him to go off without telling me."

Roger had been listening intently, frowning with the effort to understand.

"I have an idea," he said to Bill. "Ask them to come to the window."

Bill translated. Uncle Bibi and Marco followed Roger to the window.

"Tell them," Roger said, "that we have been puzzled by the light which appears in that tower every evening after dark, because we have seen, when we walked that way, that the villa is empty. Tell them that, just because we were interested and curious, we asked Italo to find out who was the owner of the house. Did he perhaps get inside, and could he have been locked in by mistake? Somebody must go there every evening if they do not live there."

Bill again translated. Marco, with an exclamation, leaned far out of the window. He drew his head in and said to Uncle Bibi, "Whether Italo is there or not, I must go to that house. It could be a spy who is signalling to the French with lights from the other side of the tower. I am not on duty again until eleven. I shall have time to go."

"Could that be Italo's secret?" Bill asked. "Could he have found out?"

"If so, he should have told me or some other Red-Shirt," Marco said.

"He may only have guessed, and wanted to make sure."

"Even so, he should have told me," Marco said sternly. "I will go now to that house. You should go home, Uncle."

"No, I am coming to see if anyone in there knows anything of Italo."

Roger said to Bill, "If Italo has got into any difficulties in that house it's our fault. I'm coming, too."

"I'm with you," Bill agreed.

Marco spoke rapidly to Bill in Italian.

"What does he say?" Roger asked.

"He asks if we have swords or pistols. He says that if there are spies in there it may be dangerous."

"No, we haven't any weapons. We can take our stout country walking sticks; that's all we've got."

The four of them went downstairs and out into the street.

Here it was much hotter than inside the house, where the shutters had been fastened over the windows all day to keep out the heat. There seemed to be no air at all in the narrow street between the tall houses. Uncle Bibi panted as he tried to keep up with the three young men. He was dreadfully worried. If Italo had somehow got inside a house which a spy was using, and had been caught there, what might the spy have done to Italo?

They were walking down the street towards the Savorelli when suddenly there was a brilliant flash of light that lit up the ruined villa. The sky above their heads seemed to burst with a great crack.

"The French guns again!" Uncle Bibi exclaimed.

"No, no," Marco answered. "It is thunder."

A second later rain was pouring down on their heads and leaping up round their ankles from the pavement. They felt as if they were walking through a sheet of water. Water soaked through their clothes and ran down from their hair into their eyes. There was another streak of lightning that lit up the dark Manselli, and again the thunder cracked above them and the sound rolled away over Rome.

"Bad luck for the illuminations," Bill muttered with his head down.

Marco said, "At least it will keep the French quiet in their tents tonight."

They tried the front gates of the Manselli, and found them locked. From down here it was not possible to see any gleam of light in the tower. The whole front of the house was dark. They could hear the rain rattling on the leaves of a tree that grew just inside the wall.

"There will be another entrance," Marco said. "Wait here till I find it. You can get some shelter from the wall."

Uncle Bibi, Roger and Bill huddled against the wall, but it gave them very little shelter from the driving rain.

Uncle Bibi spoke once. *"Signori,* I cannot help thinking what may have happened if Italo found a spy in this house, and if the spy knew that he was discovered."

"Don't think of such things," Bill said. "Italo would wriggle away like an eel if anyone caught him. He is probably now hiding somewhere inside the house and watching the spy, if there is a spy."

A fresh streak of lightning showed them the shuttered windows of the house again, and thunder rolled above them. The rain became so violent that they could no longer hear themselves speak. It seemed a very long time before Marco came back. Then they suddenly found him beside them.

"The wall is down at the side," he said. "We can get in."

They followed him round the corner to the broken place in the wall.

"You must be very careful," Marco urged. "The stones will be slippery with the wet. But I have been over. It is possible if you go slowly, feeling each step. I wish we had a lantern. Uncle, hold the tail of my shirt."

It seemed to Uncle Bibi, slipping and scrambling over the wet stones, that the tail of Marco's shirt, which he grasped firmly, was the only bit of anything solid left in the world. He slithered down on the far side, and would have fallen but for Marco's arm stopping him.

"If I find that Italo is playing about in here," Marco

said between his teeth, "I will give him such a beating!"

At last they were all four over the wall.

"At least," Marco muttered, "nobody will hear us coming in this storm."

A brilliant flash of lightning showed them the corner of the house. Then, as the thunder split the sky, it was dark again, but Marco, who seemed to be almost able to see in the dark, moved steadily forward, feeling with his hand along the wall of the house. Uncle Bibi, still holding the tail of his shirt, followed him, and the two Englishmen came behind him.

Bill began to sing softly: "Oh, 'tis my delight of a shiny night!"

"*Chut!*" Marco said sharply. Bill stopped singing.

They turned the corner of the house. Another lightning flash lit the steps up to the loggia. Marco, pulling his shirt tail out of Uncle Bibi's hand, sprang forward up the steps as the darkness closed down again. They could hear the drumming of the rain on the tiled floor of the loggia.

They could no longer see Marco.

"Let me come first," Roger pushed past Uncle Bibi and found the steps. He was up and on the floor of the loggia when he saw a thin shaft of light appear and widen across the tiled floor. Somebody was cautiously opening a door, and there was light coming from inside it.

There was a shout, and the sharp crack of a pistol shot; another shout. Roger leaned forward, grasping his stout stick, and peering into the dark. Another flash of lightning gave them a glimpse of two men in red shirts locked in a grim struggle, and rolling about on the loggia floor.

Uncle Bibi shouted, "Marco! Oh, help him, *Signori,* help him!"

In the dark and the noise of the storm it was impossible to make out where the two men were, except that once, locked together like two fighting cats, they rolled across the streak of light from the doorway.

With some idea of cutting off the enemy's retreat Bill slipped inside the door and saw that the light came from a lantern standing on the floor. He picked it up and moved cautiously to the doorway, not sure if it would help or hinder Marco to show a light suddenly on the loggia. He heard a shout from Uncle Bibi, and ran out without further hesitation, carrying the lantern. By its light he saw Marco, panting and with his shirt torn to strips, standing alone on the loggia floor.

"This one will not trouble us for the present," Marco said.

"Is he dead?" Bill asked.

"No, stunned. I banged his head on the floor."

Bill held the lantern high. Marco stepped over the body that lay huddled in the far corner.

"Take his pistol." He handed it to Roger. "We have nothing to tie this fellow up with, but it will be long enough before he stirs. Give me the lantern."

Marco led the way into the house, and the others followed him.

It was very still inside the house after the racket outside. The storm seemed to have come to an end as suddenly as it began.

"Not a sound," Marco whispered. "We must surprise them."

They stole in single file across the two rooms and began to creep up the first flight of stairs. They reached the top, crossed the first landing, and began to climb the second flight. Marco was throwing the lantern light before him, and Uncle Bibi, who came last, was almost in the dark. He stumbled over an unevenness in one step, and recovered himself.

"Quiet," Marco whispered.

They heard a footstep overhead. A voice from somewhere up above them called nervously in a low tone, "Gino? Is that you?"

Marco stopped dead and the others stopped behind him. Uncle Bibi, who was panting from the climb, felt that the noise of his breathing must sound all over the empty house.

"Is that you, Gino?" the voice called again.

Would the man above them be satisfied when there was no answer, no further sound from below, or would he come down to see? He must be listening up there in the darkness. For a minute or two they did not hear a sound. Probably he thought he had been mistaken and it was only one of those small noises that go on all the time in an empty house, for they heard footsteps again overhead and then silence.

Marco whispered, "The tower staircase will be narrow. Do not follow me too closely. He, too, will have a gun. We must not all be caught there. Take the lantern." He handed it to Bill.

Then he slipped across the landing and began cautiously to climb the stairs.

"Can't let him go alone," Roger muttered, and followed him.

Roger climbed, inwardly cursing the narrow, winding stairway, and thinking how little chance they would have if an enemy caught them there. At the last turn he saw faint light ahead. He was just behind Marco. He saw over his shoulder the tower room lit by two lanterns, one green, one red, standing on the floor by the window. A man in a red shirt was holding a third lantern, a blue one, up to the window so that its light shone out.

As Marco sprang across the room, the spy turned, gave a wordless cry of rage and fear. Marco shouted, "Benito!" Benito dropped the lantern and reached for his gun. He was too late. Marco fired; Benito slumped down on to the floor, holding his left hand to his right arm where blood sprang between his fingers.

"I might have known," Marco said, "that it would be you."

On the landing below someone began to hammer on the inside of one of the room doors. A boy's voice cried out.

"I'm here! I'm here! I'm a prisoner. Oh, come and let me out! Let me out!"

Uncle Bibi, who was just beginning to climb the stairs behind Bill, turned round and ran towards the sound. He tugged at the handle of the door, calling out, "Yes, yes, Italo, my little one. I am here; it is your old Uncle Bibi. Wait a minute, my dear, they will let you out."

Uncle Bibi, forgetting all about the possibility of an enemy with a gun, lumbered up the narrow stairs to the tower. He stopped short on the threshold of the lantern-lit room.

"Benito! Benito Lupini! But why are you here? And you are wounded. But where is the spy?"

"This is the spy," Marco said grimly.

"And we thought you were a friend," Uncle Bibi said. He added urgently, "Italo! I have found Italo! He is locked up in one of the rooms."

"Where is the key?" Marco said sternly to Benito. "Yes, we will bandage that for you before we take you to the nearest Guard House. But the key first."

"In my pocket," Benito said sullenly.

Marco, still covering him with the pistol, took the key out of Benito's pocket, and passed it to Uncle Bibi, who hurried downstairs again with Bill after him. As they unlocked and opened the door Italo threw himself into Uncle Bibi's arms and burst into tears on his shoulder.

"I thought no one would ever find me," he sobbed. "They said they would leave me here and the French would come and no one would know I was here. They only gave me one piece of bread and a cup of water all day. It was Benito. Where's Benito? Have they got him?"

"Yes, we've got him."

Benito, his arm roughly bandaged with a strip torn off Roger's shirt, came out of the opening of the tower stairway with the muzzle of Marco's pistol pressed to the back of his neck.

"I did the boy no harm," he whined. "Did I, Italo? I was only keeping him shut up out of the way till the French had come in and all fighting was over and we could all be good friends again. I didn't lay a finger on Italo, and I brought him food this morning. I was going to bring him something better this evening . . ."

"You are a spy." Italo shouted. "And this isn't the first time. It was you before at Pontevera, wasn't it? Wasn't it? You betrayed Young Italy and said it was me. Didn't you?"

"I didn't say it was you, Italo. I swear I didn't. Other people said it must be you because you were so young, and I just didn't say anything."

"It's the same thing," Italo said, sounding very like Marco. Then he added suddenly, "I'm so tired. I'm so hungry. I want to go home."

"Will you take him home, Uncle?" Marco suggested. "I will take this fellow to the nearest Guard House, and send to fetch the other downstairs. The General will deal with them in the morning."

Italo was surprised to find how weak and shaky his

legs were. But Roger and Bill each took one of his arms and walked him home between them. Uncle Bibi ran first into the house, shouting:

"Maria, Maria! Italo is here! He is safe. The poor child has been shut up in a house without food. He is starving."

"Mamma mia," Aunt Maria hurried to the kitchen and came back in a minute or two with a big bowl of hot soup full of meat and macaroni and vegetables, and thickly dusted with cheese.

Italo began to eat greedily, but he was so tired that soon he was nearly dropping asleep over it. Uncle Bibi began to tell the story to Aunt Maria; Zelinda, in her nightgown, ran in to embrace Italo and to hear what had happened.

Suddenly there was a loud knocking at the side door. Uncle Bibi went down to open it. A man in a red shirt standing there called out, "Marco? Marco Strelli? Is he here?"

"Not yet. He is coming. What is it?"

"The French are in. The sentries on the Eighteenth Bastion got so wet in the storm that they went home to put on dry clothes. The French stole up in the storm, and have occupied the Bastion. Their guns are up there pointing down into Rome. Garibaldi has summoned all men to his side to drive them out. Tell Marco to make haste. I must call others."

The Red-Shirt's footsteps went clattering away into the night.

23

Addio!

Italo woke up after a long sleep. He turned over lazily in bed. The shutters of his room were fastened across the window, so that he could not tell what time of day it was, but he had a feeling that it was not like an everyday morning when Uncle Bibi shouted to him to get up and come with him to buy fruit and vegetables from the early carts creaking into market. Today Italo knew that there was something different.

Then he remembered. He remembered with a shiver his twenty-four hours of imprisonment. He remembered with relief that he was safe home again. He remembered with glee that he had found the spy, and that Benito had cleared him of the early suspicion. Italo jumped out of bed and unfastened one of the shutters.

At this moment, Aunt Maria came into the room.

"Ah, you are awake, Italo!"

"What time is it?"

"It is afternoon, time to open the shop again after the siesta. Your uncle said that you need not do any work today. There are not many people coming for vegetables, anyhow. Everyone is too much upset. But of course you do not know."

"Know what?" Italo asked, pulling on his clothes.

"The French took possession last night of the Eighteenth Bastion. Garibaldi and the Red-Shirts counter-attacked very early this morning. You could hear the noise of the fighting from here. Ah, when I heard it I thought that no one could be left alive, that our poor Rosa would lose her Marco as we have lost our Taddeo . . ."

"Marco is all right?" Italo asked quickly.

"Yes, the Saints preserved him. Garibaldi fought like a lion at the head of the Legion. They say it is a miracle that he was preserved. His poncho was full of bullet holes. But it was all for nothing. This morning the Assembly decided to surrender. Tomorrow the French will enter Rome, and the Pope will be back here again, ruling over the city."

Italo fastened his sandals and stood up. "Come down, come down," Aunt Maria said. "I was not going to wake you so I have kept some cold meat ready for you."

"Where is Marco?"

"Garibaldi has summoned all the Red-Shirts and all those who have fought with him and would go on fighting to a meeting in St Peter's Square. Marco has just gone off there."

Aunt Maria brought a plate of cold meat and some bread and wine and oranges, and put them on the table for Italo. She went back into the kitchen.

Italo, quite restored by his long sleep, gobbled up the food, and then slipped out of the house. Uncle Bibi was busy in the shop, Aunt Maria in the kitchen, Zelinda was at school. Since he need not work today, Italo thought he would go and see what was happening in the square. Even his twenty-four hours' imprisonment in the Manselli had not cured him of wanting to know about things.

The shops were just opening again after the siesta as

154

Italo ran through the hot streets, where already the sun had dried up every trace of last night's storm.

When he came out of one of the side streets leading into the big square in front of St Peter's, he was astonished. The whole square seemed to be a sea of Red-Shirts. There was a carriage in the middle with no horses harnessed to it. As Italo watched a man climbed up to stand on the box of the carriage. The crowd in the square began to cheer as if they would shout the sky down. Italo cheered, too, for of course he knew that face and the poncho and the sombrero, even before Garibaldi's voice rang out over the square.

"The Assembly have sent their surrender to the French," Garibaldi shouted. "But I do not surrender. The Legion does not surrender. I am leaving Rome to carry on the war for the freedom of Italy. Whoever is willing to follow me will be received among my people. I ask nothing from you but love of your country. You will have no pay and no rest. You will have bread and water where you chance to find any. Anyone who is not satisfied with such a life had better remain behind. Once you have passed through the gates of Rome every step backwards is towards death."

Again the cheers rang out.

"I ask for volunteers," Garibaldi cried.

The first to come forward was his wife, Anita, dressed like one of his soldiers in trousers and a red shirt. One by one the others followed her, saluting the General as they passed the carriage, and ranging themselves in a block on the far side of the square.

Italo pressed nearer in his excitement. He followed a stream of Red-Shirts in front of him. He must volunteer! Of course he must volunteer! He belonged to Young Italy, he had just caught a spy; he was quite old enough. He was falling into the line that was going to pass the carriage when a voice above him said, "Italo!"

He looked up and saw Marco riding a gray horse. He had just time to wonder where Marco had got the gray horse from, when Marco swung himself down from the saddle and took him by the arm.

"Italo, what are you doing here?"

"I'm going to volunteer."

"No, you are not. You are not old enough yet for what we shall have to do. There will be long forced marches and battles. We cannot take children, they would hamper us."

Italo said defiantly, "Anyhow, I caught a spy."

"I know you did. The General knows it. But you must not get in the way now."

"Marco, what happened to Benito?"

"He was shot, and the other one, Gino, this morning." Marco added, "I was sorry that Benito came from Pontevera. Say a prayer for his mother, Italo."

"Let me, let me come with you, Marco," Italo begged.

"No," Marco answered. "You must let me go. You must go back to Uncle Bibi, and be a son to him since he has lost Taddeo. But when you can, go down to the farm and embrace our mother and Papa for me."

"Where are you going? When will you come back?"

"I don't know. I shall follow where Garibaldi leads us."

Marco suddenly stooped and kissed his young brother on both cheeks.

"*Addio,* Italo. I will send you word when I can. In a few years you will be old enough to join us. Meanwhile watch, wait, listen, in case there is anything you can do to help one of us. Remember that you have taken the oath and are just as much one of Young Italy as if you were riding out with us. You and I are brothers twice over since we have both taken the twig of cypress. *Ora e sempre*. Now and for always."

Marco mounted again, and rode forward towards Garibaldi. Italo turned to go home.

Aftermath

Garibaldi and his volunteers rode out of Rome by the Porta San Giovanni only an hour or two before the French re-occupied the city. Thenceforth they had a very hard time, as Garibaldi had foreseen: they managed to make their way north, in spite of the hostile Neapolitan and French armies behind them, and the Austrians in front. They had no supplies; there were many desertions. Finally they were obliged to disband, and Garibaldi himself went into exile.

But that was not the end of the story of the *Risorgimento*. Within less than ten years the King of Piedmont —partly stirred by his own ambitions—was trying to reduce foreign rule in northern Italy; and in 1860 Garibaldi landed in southern Italy to lead the famous expedition of the Thousand. They conquered the island of Sicily and then went on to the mainland to take the kingdom of Naples (where the Strelli held their farmstead). King Victor of Piedmont now marched down from the north to become—with Garibaldi's agreement —the King of a new Italy.

There were still a few exceptions to this unification: Venice was brought in as the result of a war in 1866; but the great exception—Rome itself—had to wait until 1870. Then the French were forced to withdraw all their forces from the city because of a war nearer home: this was Italy's opportunity, and Rome was taken, to become at last the capital of the new, united, free country. The dream of Garibaldi and so many other Italians was realized.

DATE DUE

SEP 26 '83			
GAYLORD			PRINTED IN U.S.A.